EDWARD A. GRAINGER'S
CASH LARAMIE & GIDEON MILES SERIES

THE GUNS OF VEDAUWOO

as written by
WAYNE D. DUNDEE

ISBN: 978-0-9912039-3-2

BEAT to a PULP
PO Box 173
Freeville, New York 13068
USA
Email: btapzine@beattoapulp.com
Visit us at www.beattoapulp.com

This is for Richard Prosch, who introduced me
to Vedauwoo.

—WD—

It was a cool, clear, early fall afternoon when Deputy U.S. Marshal Cash Laramie arrived back in Cheyenne with his prisoner, Luther Hyatt, in tow.

The pair rode directly to the back side of the federal building, where there was a rear entrance to the holding cells down in the basement. This entrance was the one commonly used by lawmen delivering prisoners to the lockup.

Cash had been on the trail with Hyatt for three days, leaving him weary, irritable, and anxious to get the suspected killer off his hands. Hyatt was a slovenly, heavy-gutted individual. Foul-tempered, foul-smelling, and foul-mouthed. Charged with butchering an entire family up north near Devil's Tower. Those who'd seen what was left of his alleged victims were quick to offer the opinion that whoever was responsible must have been spawned by the very demon that fabled landmark was named after. Cash didn't know about that but, after spending time in the company of the surly, unrepentant Hyatt, he had little doubt of the man's guilt. A trial was yet to be held, but Cash felt confident a hangman's noose would be the end result and, as far as he was concerned, it couldn't fall around this man's neck soon enough.

After dismounting and tying both horses—his own pinto and Hyatt's blaze-face, which Cash had been leading—to a hitch rail, the marshal stepped over and slammed the heavy metal knocker several times against the outside of the door leading down to the holding cells. This signaled whatever jailers were on duty inside that a new prisoner was ready to be brought down.

Without waiting for the jailers to respond, Cash returned to the horses and reached up to unfasten Hyatt so he could climb down out of the saddle. The prisoner's wrists were handcuffed in front of him, with an additional set of cuffs wrapped around the linking chain and then ratcheted tightly to the saddle horn. This kept Hyatt secured in place, allowing him to sit his saddle in reasonable comfort yet denying him any control over his horse and thereby no chance to try and bolt free.

Before unlocking the manacles clamped around the saddle horn, Cash aimed a dark scowl up at the mounted man and said, "You get a notion to try anything funny, I won't hesitate to drop you right here in the dust. Understood?"

"You're supposed to be deliverin' me for a fair trial," said Hyatt. "Not bring me all this way only to threaten gunnin' me down like a dog in the street."

"Consider yourself delivered. Up to you to call the tune on how it plays from here." Cash unfastened the manacles and unwrapped them from the cuffs still clamped to Hyatt's wrists. "And comparin' yourself to a dog," he added, "is an insult to even the mangiest cur I ever saw."

"Yeah, you'd know all about dogs, wouldn't you?" Hyatt sneered. "Bein' raised by injuns the way you was, you probably even *et* your share."

"When that lockup door opens in a minute, there are two ways to go down the steps leading to your cell," Cash advised him. "You can walk down, or you can get *dragged* down. You keep runnin' your mouth and aggravatin' me, you won't be in any shape to make the trip on your feet. And I've seen those jailers drag other fellas down. Trust me, they don't like the extra work so they tend to do it with a sort of chip on their shoulders. That means they got a bad habit of letting the thick, stupid skull of whoever it is they're draggin' bounce real careless-like on each and every step— sometimes more than once."

Hyatt's sneer stretched wider. "You don't scare me with that kind of talk. You're just stung because I spoke bad about your precious injun mongrels. I forgot the other thing you heathen redskins do with your dogs—tell me, how hard was it to fight off your daddy and brothers for the chance to claim the prettiest bitch in the litter so you could have your turn at fornicat—"

Cash grabbed him by his belt and one arm and jerked outward with a snarling curse. He lifted the prisoner out of his stirrups, hoisting him momentarily above his head, and then hurled the man to the ground like a sack of potatoes.

Hyatt landed with a loud *hawff!* Air and spittle gushed from his mouth. He squirmed on the ground momentarily before trying to push to his hands and knees. Cash was on him in an instant. A booted toe crashed into stomach and ribs and sent Hyatt rolling lumpily away.

Cash went after him, reaching down to grab his shirtfront with the intent of hauling him up so he could knock him back down again. But Hyatt had more fight left in him than Cash expected. When the marshal leaned over, Hyatt lunged to meet him, swinging both fists upward with the handcuff chain stretched taut between them. The chain clipped Cash hard under the point of his chin, jolting him, sending him staggering backward.

At this moment, the heavy door to the lockup swung open and two uniformed jailers appeared in the doorway. One of the men had some years on him and sported bristly mutton-chop sideburns shot with gray; the other was younger, somewhat gawky in appearance, and clean-shaven. Seeing what was happening, the younger man immediately reached for the billy club hanging from a loop on his thick uniform belt.

The older jailer promptly clamped a restraining grip on his partner's wrist. "Hold on there, Bindley me lad. Don't get too excited."

"But that prisoner's trying to escape," Bindley, the young jailer, wailed. "He's fighting the marshal—we need to lend a hand!"

"Don't you recognize who that marshal is?"

"I've only been working here for a couple of weeks," Bindley reminded him. "I don't recognize all the different law officers by sight yet."

"Well, see to it you remember this one," advised the older guard, whose name was O'Shea. "That scrapper there is none other than Cash Laramie."

"The one they call the Outlaw Marshal?"

"Some do. Not me," O'Shea was quick to respond. "His ways may be rough, true. But nobody who plays straight with the law has got a concern from him, says I. And the day Cash Laramie can't handle the likes of that scruffy clod he's mixin' with there, well, I'm after thinkin' today won't be that day. So just sit tight for a minute, lad, and enjoy the show."

After Hyatt's surprise blow stunned him and sent him reeling, Cash had barely managed to stay on his feet. In the time it took for him to regain his balance and get his head cleared, Hyatt was up and charging straight for him, swinging his doubled fists in a roundhouse blow meant to finish the marshal right then and there. Cash could have gone for the Colt holstered on his hip, but he rejected resorting to that as quickly as the thought flashed through his mind. No, by God, he'd started this fracas with his two bare hands and that's the way he would end it. At the last instant, Cash was able to twist away and take Hyatt's menacing punch only grazingly off the top of his head. But the momentum of Hyatt's bull-like charge carried him forward and still brought him crashing against the marshal, his shoulder driving hard into Cash's chest. Both men tumbled to the ground, tangled together, pummeling and kicking and cursing.

It was Cash's misfortune to end up on the bottom of the tangle. He tried to flail his way clear but couldn't get enough leverage into his punches to succeed. Hyatt bore down on him relentlessly, grinding him into the ground. And then the prisoner suddenly reared back and swung his doubled fists again. This time they found their target solidly, hammering against Cash's jaw. With an enraged grunt, the heavier man followed up by lurching forward again, once more separating his fists as far as their restraining chain would allow and then slamming the chain down across Cash's throat. Hyatt leaned into the choke with all his strength and weight, the links of the chain chewing flesh and threatening to pulverize Cash's windpipe.

Cash struggled in vain. Stars and black spots whirled in his vision.

Desperately, he reached up with both hands and sank his thumbs deep into Hyatt's eye sockets. The prisoner howled and tried to pull his head away but, in addition to his gouging thumbs, Cash's fingers were ensnarled in the long, greasy hair spilling around Hyatt's face. He gripped the man's head tightly between his palms, jerking, twisting, not allowing it to pull free. All the while he kept digging his thumbs deeper.

Finally, with a roar or pain and rage, Hyatt released the pressure of the chain on Cash's throat and pitched his body to one side, breaking the claw-like grip of the marshal's hands. He toppled to the ground and tried to roll clear. But Cash wasted no time scrambling after him. Even though he was coughing and sucking for air, he sensed he now had the advantage over the nearly-blinded Hyatt and he wasn't about to give it up. When the prisoner rose to his knees, Cash, also on his knees, stretched out and threw a hard, lightning-fast right hook. He immediately followed that with a left hook. Hyatt wavered limply, ready to go down. Cash cocked a fist once more, measuring his man, and then finished him with a snapping right cross that sprawled Hyatt flat on his back.

Cash rocked back on his haunches, fighting to catch his breath. He sleeved stinging sweat from his eyes and then his hand went to his throat, first to make sure the arrowhead that hung around his neck on a leather thong was intact and undamaged and then to gingerly touch his throat where the handcuff chain had chewed the skin raw. When he pulled his hand away and looked down at it, the fingertips were smeared with blood.

O'Shea and Bindley, the two jailers, came walking over.

Cash turned his head and looked up at them. "What the hell's the story with you two? You afraid of gettin' scratches on those shiny billy clubs you're apparently carryin' around for decoration?"

"Aw, come on, Cash," O'Shea protested. "The way you and him was all scrambled together, what chance did we have of trying to get a lick in at him without the risk of hitting you?" His mouth fell into a lopsided grin. "Besides, I had nary a doubt who was going to come out on top."

"Well, I'm glad *you* were so damn sure of the outcome," Cash grumbled. "From the view I had, it was lookin' mighty touch-and-go there for a minute."

O'Shea stretched out a hand and Cash grasped it, accepting the assistance in rising to his feet.

"What's the name of our scrappy new guest?" O'Shea inquired.

"Luther Hyatt, best get him downstairs and get him locked behind bars before his scrappiness kicks in again."

O'Shea nodded. "Aye, that we'll do. Come on, Bindley me lad. Give me a hand and we'll be after depositing this fella where he'll be able to do no more harm—either to himself or anybody else."

Each of the jailers took a leg and unceremoniously began dragging Hyatt across the ground, in the direction of the door to the lockup.

"Be careful with him," Cash cautioned. He leaned over to reclaim the black Stetson that had been knocked from his head during the scuffle, slapped it against his leg to knock off some of the added dust.

"We'll do our best," O'Shea grunted. "But this is a good-sized fella we got hold of here, and you know how hard it is to maneuver inside that narrow stairwell."

Cash displayed one of his rare smiles—as thin and cold as a wolf's. "What I meant," he said, "was be careful you don't miss hitting any of the steps with his head on the way down."

2

Cash took time to stable the horses and stow his trail gear before returning to the lockup for the sake of officially signing over custody of his prisoner. O'Shea had the necessary paperwork ready and he also had something else—a message for Cash.

"Chief Penn is wanting to see you, Cash. Sent down one of the courthouse clerks with word for you to come to his office 'posthaste.'"

Cash swore under his breath. "How'd he hear so quick I was even back in town?"

"Can't say. Only know the message that was delivered."

Cash straightened up from signing the papers. He grimaced. "Posthaste, eh?"

"The very words."

Since it was so late in the day and he was coming off a long stretch out on the trail, a visit with Chief Marshal Devon Penn hadn't exactly been part of Cash's plans for how he aimed to spend the balance of the afternoon and evening. A hot bath, a sit-down meal, some top-shelf libation to cut the trail dust, and an energetic romp (or two) with Lenora Wilkes, his favorite soiled dove, were more the kinds of thing he'd had in mind. He'd figured checking in with his superior could wait until morning, especially since he had nothing of any significance to report, other than he'd brought back Hyatt, as he was assigned to do.

The fact Penn had not only sent for him but had added a sense of urgency told Cash this clearly had to be something more than just a cordial welcome back to town.

"Before you head on up there, though," O'Shea added, "you ought to take care of your throat, the way that handcuff chain tore hell out it." He gestured toward a small alcove opposite the row of heavily-barred cells. Back there was a table and a pair of straight-backed chairs, a small stove with a coffee pot perched on top of it, and a wash basin on a stand in front of a piece of mirror hanging on the wall. "I had Bindley fetch a fresh pail of water for the basin in there and I laid out some clean towels. You go ahead and wash up, clean your wounds. Then I can have a look at 'em if you want. There's some gauze bandages in a drawer in there somewhere if we need to do some patchin' up."

"Obliged." Cash went into the alcove, poured some of the fresh water, stripped off his jacket and shirt then worked up a good lather getting washed. The muscles under the taut skin of his shoulders and back rippled smoothly. He was a trim, broad-shouldered six-footer and even in the mundane act of getting washed up there was an aura of barely restrained energy about him, like a compressed spring ready to be released or a coiled whip waiting to lash out.

Once the sweat and grime were rinsed away, the abrasions on his neck were red and raw, but the skin wasn't broken very deeply and the bleeding had stopped. Cash decided no bandages were necessary. He settled instead for giving his neckerchief a quick rinse and, after squeezing it dry and tying it back in place along with the arrowhead dangling on its thong, the scrapes to his neck were barely visible.

"Good as new," O'Shea announced when he was done. "And don't go worryin' after your newly-delivered prisoner, either. As soon as he wakes up, I'll see to it he has a chance to get cleaned up as well—I'll slosh your used wash-water on him."

* * *

Chief U.S. Marshal Devon Penn sat behind his desk, elbows resting on its polished top, sausage-thick fingers steepled before his round face. "We have a situation," he was explaining. "Certain incidents have occurred recently that, if added together in just the right way, could amount to a veritable powder keg primed for somebody to light the fuse."

Cash was seated on the front side of the desk, slouched in the comfortable confines of one of two Windsor Armchairs that Penn had available for visitors. A thin cheroot—unlighted in deference to Penn's well-known dislike for tobacco smoke clouding his office—was clenched between his teeth. "We're pretty good at pinchin' off fuses," he replied, almost nonchalantly. "When we can't, we're good at cleanin' up the mess after the explosion goes off."

Penn looked anguished. "Well, let's hope to hell this is one of those times we can pinch off the fuse. That's why I was relieved to hear you were back in town and why I promptly sent for you. I know you just got in off the trail and rate a well-deserved rest, but I'm afraid I have to ask you to turn around and ride back out again almost immediately."

"Won't be the first time." Cash shrugged fatalistically. "So how about we quit talkin' in generalities and get to some details—exactly what is this fuse I'm supposed to ride out and pinch off? Or, more importantly I guess, what makes up the potential powder keg it's attached to?"

Penn leaned back in his chair, emitting a raged sigh. "No doubt you've heard of the Ghost Dance movement that is spreading through several of the Indian tribes?"

Cash narrowed his eyes and gave a measured nod. "Heard of it. Hard to believe so many are takin' it so serious."

The Ghost Dance movement—or religion, many were calling it—had first been introduced nearly twenty years ago in the Paiute Nation. In that early incarnation, it amounted to a fairly benign concept of earth renewal and a reintroduction of ancient spiritual teachings. More recently, however, a new messiah, a powerful Northern Paiute medicine man named Wovoka, had introduced a new element to the movement after claiming he'd had a prophetic vision during a solar eclipse. In Wovoka's vision he saw a great awakening of all Indian Nations, including the resurrection of the dead, and the withdrawal of all whites— if Indians lived righteously and ritualistically performed a circle dance known as the Ghost Dance in a recurring series of 5-day-long gatherings. Originally starting with the Paiutes in Nevada, the revitalized movement had caught on like wild fire and now Ghost Dances were being performed on reservations all across the West by tribes of all Nations.

"But to my understanding," Cash went on, "the great awakening this Ghost Dance is supposed to bring about will all take place peaceably, without violence or threat."

Penn nodded. "That was according to Wovoka's original vision and teachings, true enough. But, as the movement spreads, there are signs not everybody sees it quite that way. Ever hear of a Sioux sub-chief and half-assed holy man named Kicking Bear?"

"Can't say I have."

"Well, among other things, he's pretty tight with ol' Sitting Bull over on the Pine Ridge Reservation in Nebraska. They fought at Little Big Horn together. Not so long ago, it seems Sitting Bull sent him out to Nevada to meet with Wovoka, to find out more about the Ghost Dance and bring back what he learned." Penn frowned and gave a disapproving shake of his head that caused the fleshy pouch of his double chin to quiver faintly. "What Kicking Bear came back with, unfortunately, was an interpretation to Wovoka's prophecy that added a new feature—something he's calling a Ghost Shirt, a shirt that has the magical power to turn away the white man's bullets."

"Why need something like that if the whole aim of the Dance is peaceful change?"

"That's exactly what has got a lot of Army brass and the Bureau of Indian Affairs folks so concerned. Part of the Ghost Dance awakening calls for a renewed land where all evil has been purged away. If Kicking Bear's notion about bullet-turning Ghost Shirts starts to spread more widely through all the ceremonies already taking place, you can see where that might add a whole new wrinkle. Cause you to wonder what if some of the followers began seeing that 'purging out evil' part as a call to once again try driving out the white man, only this time with a magic garment that gives protection against his bullets."

13

"An uprising, you mean."

"Be no other word for it."

Cash frowned. "Gotta say, that sounds like a bit of a stretch to me. More than I guess it does to you. But, either way, how does it concern the Marshals service? You said the Army and the Bureau of Indian Affairs are already alerted— aren't they the ones who need to stay on top of it?"

"For that part of the matter, to be sure," Penn answered. "However, you'll recall I also said there were incidents, plural, that factor into this potential powder keg. The one that more directly concerns us has to do with a prison break that occurred down at Castle Rock Prison, south of Denver, two days ago. One of the escapees was a half breed named Vilo Creed. Ever hear of him?"

"Creed the Breed," Cash muttered. "Sounds like the villain out of some cheap penny dreadful. But no, I never heard of anybody by that name in real life."

Penn grunted. "By all accounts, Creed is certainly a villain. And the crimes that put him behind bars were surely dreadful enough. It's unfortunate he's *not* merely a work of fiction." The chief marshal reached out and tapped a pudgy forefinger down onto a sheaf of papers that lay on the desktop. "There are details on Creed's background in here, telegraphed to me by the Colorado authorities. Along with those of another man named Harley Boyd."

"I take it the Colorado authorities have reason to think those boys are headed our way?"

"Only Creed. Boyd might've started out this way, since he was part of the prison break, too. But he didn't make it far. The prison posse who rode out in pursuit found what was left of him on the trail. He'd been savagely beaten and sliced up with a knife. Tortured. Whoever did it, left him for dead. But he wasn't. Not quite. He lived long enough to wheeze out three words after the posse came upon him. 'Creed … guns … Vedauwoo.' That's all he had left in him before he succumbed."

"So Creed was the one who tortured him."

"Not much doubt."

"Okay. That explains why he included Creed in his final words. And I know where Vedauwoo is, so that must be where Boyd figures Creed is headed for. But how does mention of guns fit in?"

Penn tapped the sheaf of papers again. "You got to back up to Boyd's history. He went to prison in 1875 for killing a Denver businessman over a watch. But before that he'd long been suspected of running guns to the Indians. Only nobody could ever gather enough proof to bring charges.

"Less than two months before his arrest for the Denver murder, Boyd was again suspected of being part of a gang— maybe the leader—who robbed a shipment of arms bound for Fort Collins. They got away with one hundred Springfield Model 1873 carbines. But again, nothing could be proven against Boyd. Several other men who were also suspected of being part of the gang ended up dead in only a matter of days after the robbery—two died shooting it out with authorities attempting to bring them in for questioning; three others were found murdered without apparent motive."

"Boyd cleaning house," Cash said. "Making sure no one was left who might cave and spill his name as part of the deal."

"That was the general belief. But, once more, no proof. What's more, there's no evidence of the stolen guns ever having been delivered to any of the Indian tribes who were raising so much hell during that time. No delivery to the Indians, no delivery anywhere else—at least not as far as anybody has ever been able to determine."

"So Boyd stashed 'em somewhere while the heat was turned up high, while he was clearing the slate of anybody who could point back to him. But then, before he could haul the rifles out again in order to try and make his sale, he was stupid enough to get in a fight over a watch and end up convicted for murder."

"His luck finally ran out."

Cash shook his head. "Had nothing to do with luck. Like I said, he was stupid."

Penn shrugged indifferently. "Okay, I'll concede you that. But when he got crossways of Creed, *that* sure as hell turned out to be bad luck for Boyd."

"How does Creed figure in on the gun angle?"

"He was Boyd's cellmate for the past two months," Penn explained. "Stubborn damn Boyd would never admit a peep about having anything to do with that arms robbery, not even when the prison board offered him a deal on his murder sentence if he'd cooperate and turn over the guns. But with Creed, his cellmate who was scheduled for a trip to the gallows, he apparently talked more freely."

"Was Creed the one behind the prison break?"

"They're still trying to figure that out. About twenty prisoners made it free. They scattered into a half dozen different groups once they were out and, as far as anyone can tell so far, there's no link between the different groups. Last I heard—and I'm getting telegram updates daily—all the prison authorities can say right now is that some kind of explosive charge was set at one of the side gates and a food delivery wagon somehow set it off when it tried to pass through. All hell broke loose and the twenty escapees used the chaos and confusion to make their break."

"I take it Creed and Boyd were one of the 'groups' who split away once they were out. Just the two of 'em?"

"The way it looks."

"Okay, but I still don't—" Cash hesitated for a moment, looking thoughtful. He removed the cheroot from the corner of his mouth. When he spoke again his words came in less of a rush. "I was about to say I didn't see why anybody would be in a hurry to get their hands on those stolen Springfields after all this time, considerin' how outdated they are and how the Indian wars are over and all. Can't think of a ready buyer unless maybe you hauled 'em all the way down to Mexico. But with this Ghost Shirt business coming to a simmer practically in our back yard, the sudden availability of that many rifles just might be all it'd take to bring the pot to a boil. That what you're thinkin'?"

"You got it. And here's the clincher: Creed's Indian bloodline is Lakota Sioux. Same as Kicking Bear. Sitting Bull, too, for that matter—but the old chief doesn't seem to figure into any of this except for finding the whole Ghost Dance thing an amusing way to annoy the white man.

"At any rate, Creed's been heard to brag he's shirttail kin to Kicking Bear. Probably not something Kicking Bear'd be likely to brag about in return, even if it was true. Not before, anyway, not with Creed's low reputation. But now, if Kicking Bear was to all of a sudden learn he had a mixed blood cousin who could hand over a hundred rifles right at the time he was stirring up a bunch of hot bloods with his

17

Ghost Shirt interpretation of the new Indian Nation awakening …"

"Outside news spreads fast through a prison," Cash mused, "especially news about something that's giving fits to the authorities. Not much doubt that Creed, Boyd, and the other inmates would have heard about the whole Ghost Dance-Ghost Shirt thing."

"You see what I mean about a powder keg forming if these individual pieces start falling together?"

"Sure do," Cash said in a low voice. "If Boyd stashed the stolen guns in Vedauwoo, like his final words imply, then Creed is on his way there to claim 'em after torturing Boyd to get their exact location out of him. That means somebody needs to beat Creed there and stop him before he digs 'em up and fans the flames of an uprising even more by making 'em available to Kicking Bear and the Ghost Shirt hot bloods."

"You know Vedauwoo as well or better than any man I've got. The timing of you returning to town when you did could hardly have been better."

"Yeah. Lucky me," Cash said dryly.

"There's no telling how quickly Creed will try to make it there. He may go straightaway, he may take time to try and round up some others to accompany him. The prison break was two days ago, as I said. It seems likely Creed would need at least a little while to gather some supplies and a wagon or pack horses to bring out the guns. But if he made a beeline straight for it, he could already be there."

"We can't take the chance. I need to head for Vedauwoo right away."

"I've already got men out on a train robbery that took place up north night before last, and others assigned to a bloody range war farther west. I'm sorry I don't have anybody else available to send with you."

"Not the first time for that, either," Cash said resignedly. He rose up out of his chair and reached for the sheaf of papers Penn had prepared for him.

"I won't have any way to stay in contact with you in case anything changes," Penn said. "Like I told you, I'm getting regular updates from the Colorado authorities. There's always the chance—a slim one, I'm afraid—they might catch up with Creed before he even makes it up here to our neck of the woods. We'll give it a week. If he hasn't shown up in Vedauwoo by then, I want you to hightail it back here and we'll reassess how things stand."

"A week should do it," Cash agreed.

"You watch your ass out there," Penn said. He pointed toward the papers Cash had picked up. "You scan through those, you'll see quick enough what a nasty bastard this Creed is. Stay extra sharp when it comes to him, you hear?"

3

Once again mounted on Paint, his tall pinto stallion, and leading a buckskin pack horse, Cash rode out the next day at first light.

The pack horse had been supplied and provisioned by Chief Marshal Penn, who took care of all arrangements the previous evening in order to allow Cash a measure of free time to see to his own affairs. Cash used the opportunity to fit in the bath and hot meal he'd been looking forward to, as well as an enjoyable dalliance with Lenora. None of it was as completely satisfying as it might have been, however, not with the specter of Vilo Creed and the looming threat of a potential Indian uprising weighing on his mind throughout. Nevertheless, he'd managed a stretch of restful sleep during the overnight hours and woke feeling refreshed and resolved to the task ahead.

Now, out in the crisp morning air, the breath from himself and the horses streaming out in vapor trails caught by the brilliant wash of the new day, he was glad to be underway. His destination lay due west across a span of rolling, mostly treeless terrain. Clumps of yucca and sage dotted the rise and fall of stubborn, brownish-green grass, broken occasionally by ragged rock outcroppings and now and then a low, flat mesa. As he rode, Cash was always in sight of hazy humps off to his left, the northern reaches of the Colorado Rockies; ahead, from the higher slopes, he could also see the purplish ridges of the Laramies and the Snowy Range in the distance.

It would take the better part of a day's ride to reach Vedauwoo.

The Vedauwoo Rocks—called Skull Rocks by some— were a spectacular concentration of hills and rock outcropping that thrust abruptly up out of the high plains landscape almost like an abbreviated mountain range in their own right. Steep granite peaks reached hundreds of feet into the sky, some ending in jagged fingers, others blunted and broken, leaving massive tumbled boulders strewn across the inter-mingled hills overgrown with fir and aspen and cut by streams and sharp, narrow canyons. It was a distinctly beautiful area that Cash had warm personal memories of and always enjoyed returning to … at least, he always had in the past.

Raised from infancy to the age of twelve by a band of Arapaho under the leadership of Lightning Cloud, his adoptive father, Cash had hunted the trails and fished the streams of Vedauwoo throughout much of his boyhood. He had killed his first elk and had first met the challenge of a cougar there. From their village to the north and east, his tribe's hunting parties often sought out the bounty of Vedauwoo's myriad wildlife to supplement the buffalo of the open prairie. And each spring it was home to spiritual ceremonies of great significance. The name Vedauwoo, in fact, was derived from the old-tongue "*bito'o'wu*," meaning "earth-born," and had long been recognized by the Arapaho as a special place, one to be revered.

After the death of his Arapaho mother, Elina, Cash's tribe made the decision to migrate north to Canada, away from the rapidly advancing tide of America's western expansion and the changes it was forcing on the native people in its path. The time had also been right for Cash to part ways with the Arapaho and seek his path in the White World, to which he'd initially been born. Without the loving, patient hand of Elina to steady him and to balance his oft-times contentious relationship with Lightning Cloud, life in the tribe would have been difficult if not impossible.

It had been Elina who'd taken him in, a mere infant plucked from the gunsmoke-shrouded Fall Creek battlefield after his white birth parents had been killed in a crossfire between Arapaho and Cavalry combatants. It had been Elina who'd nursed and nurtured him and then, as he grew, insisted he be accepted as part of the tribe; Lightning Cloud had gone along with her wishes—had even done his part in teaching the boy the ways of a man and a warrior, bestowing upon him the Arapaho name White Deer—because of his love and devotion to his wife. With Elina gone, however, it was clear that White Deer's future lay elsewhere.

Cash couldn't help thinking of these things now, as he rode once more toward Vedauwoo. His hand involuntarily touched the arrowhead hanging about his neck, a parting gift from his dying mother. In his mind's eye he could clearly see her lovely face and hear her final soft words and he once again felt a pang of the emptiness that had been a part of him ever since her passing. But, for the most part, when he thought back on his time with the Arapaho, he seldom allowed himself to dwell on the sadder, harsher aspects of those years. He'd long ago put that part of his life in proper perspective, taking away only the positives—the unconditional love he'd received from Elina, the strengths and skills he had learned from Lightning Cloud.

Besides, he reminded himself now, what he needed to stay focused on at the moment was the pending potential confrontation with Vilo Creed. He'd read through the papers Penn had furnished him—consisting of past wanted posters the chief marshal had dug out of the files, along with additional newer details supplied via telegram updates from the authorities down in Colorado—and it was quickly obvious that Creed was a cold-blooded, merciless, unpredictable, thoroughly dangerous individual. Murder, rape, armed robbery, blackmail, arson, kidnapping ... there wasn't much in the way of violent crime his name hadn't been linked to. Too seldom, unfortunately (same as had been the case for his cellmate Harley Boyd), accompanied by enough proof to put him behind bars except for brief stints. What had finally landed him in prison awaiting his turn on the gallows was the slaughter of five prostitutes and three of their customers—everyone who'd been present in the brothel where Creed went crazy from an over indulgence of too-green alcohol that sent him on a demon-vision killing spree followed by an attempt to burn down the establishment in the aftermath. The clincher had been the fact that one of the victims left in his wake had been the son of a prominent politician.

Cash wondered, with bitter sarcasm, if Creed had only killed and burned the whores, would he still have been sentenced to hang? Or might he instead have gotten off with mere incarceration? The justice handed out for killing the likes of whores and for killing the likes of a powerful politician's son often tended to be very different things.

Except Cash wasn't inclined to see those kinds of differences. Which was why he had a tendency for sometimes meting out his own brand of justice … and that, in turn, was why there were those who referred to him as "the Outlaw Marshal."

* * *

Jack Sampson swallowed a gulp of bitter coffee and wished he had some sugar to put in it. Sampson wished for many things in his life. But, because he was lazy and shiftless (and knew it), he settled for very little.

Sampson looked about him now at the interior of the cracked, crumbling adobe shell left from what had once been a sturdy military-style blockhouse. The structure was one of the few buildings still standing within the ruins of Fort Vasquez, an old fur trading post just off the front range of the Colorado Rockies. The post had been abandoned decades ago, its walls left to collapse and become overgrown with weeds and tangled brush. Since there was nobody around to say otherwise, Sampson had moved into these ruins the previous spring. With winter coming on, he'd made a few half-hearted attempts to patch the cracks in the walls with mud and straw and some old, half-rotted planks he'd found lying around. But the place would still leak like a sieve when the cold winds came roaring down out of the mountains. And the makeshift stove in the middle of the room sure as hell wasn't going to be able to throw out enough offsetting heat … even if he ever got around to chopping and storing enough wood to keep it fueled.

Sampson took another drink of coffee but the hot liquid wasn't enough to stop the shiver that ran through him at the thought of oncoming winter. Sampson was a slight man with quick, jerky movements, presently wrapped in a ratty old wool coat that made him appear considerably bulkier than he really was. His wiry black hair and broad, flat face, however, did nothing to mask the mixture of Negro and Sioux blood that coursed through his veins.

The rear portion of the room where Sampson sat was sectioned off by a row of buffalo hides hanging from a hemp rope stretched taut between the walls. This created a measure of privacy for the sleeping quarters located on the other side.

As Sampson poured himself more coffee, he heard the sound of a heavy body stirring behind the buffalo hide curtain. That would be Creed, Sampson told himself. Once again he shivered, and this time it had nothing to do with the thought of cold weather coming on.

A minute later, two of the buffalo hides parted and Creed emerged from the sleeping area. He was not a tall man, less than six feet in height, but possessed massive shoulders and a barrel chest. An unruly shock of straight, tar-black hair spilled over his eyes and trailed down the back of his neck. Under shaggy brows his eyes were fierce and restless and glistened with a bright, brittle blackness all their own.

With a thick-fingered hand as broad as a frying pan, Creed shoved hair back away from his eyes and said, "I thought I smelled coffee cooking." He gestured toward the pot on the makeshift stove. "You got another cup?"

Sampson reached down to rummage in a wooden box setting beside the sawed-off section of log he was seated on. He pulled out a dented tin cup and placed it on the rough-hewn, lopsided table at which he sat. Creed took the cup and poured it full of coffee from the pot on the stove.

"Stout-looking brew," Creed observed, regarding the steaming contents of the cup.

"Yeah, I guess it is. Sorry I don't have no sugar or nothing to put in it," Sampson said.

"No problem. I like my coffee straight and strong." Creed took a big gulp, seemingly oblivious to the heat of the liquid. Lowering the cup, he smacked his lips and said, "Yeah, that's more like it. In that shithole prison, they fed us watered-down coffee that wasn't even hot. More like warmed over piss."

Sampson stood up. "That pot's probably getting low, ain't it? Go ahead and refill your cup, I'll brew another."

Creed nodded. "That'd be good. I like the smell of coffee brewing almost as much as I like drinking it."

Creed topped off his cup and then found another sawed-off section of log to sit down on while Sampson went about making a fresh pot.

"The smell of that first pot cooking up before was especially welcome," Creed said, "because it helped offset the smell of your woman back there." He jabbed a thick thumb toward the sleeping area behind the buffalo hides. "Damn, man, I hate to sound ungrateful for the hospitality of letting me have a roll with her and all. But you need to drag her and a bar of soap to the nearest creek and hold her ass down until the suds quit foaming. She is some kind of ripe!"

"I reckon," Sampson shrugged indifferently, "but she don't complain much and she fetches a decent meal out of whatever vittles I manage to scrape together. Plus, with the nights getting colder, she makes a right nice belly warmer."

Creed grunted. "Yeah, I can see where that big old ass of hers would be good for keeping a fella right toasty on a cold night. Forget I said anything. She's your woman, you make do with her however you see fit. And I *am* grateful for you letting me roll with her last night … Lord knows, it'd been a long damn stretch since I had me a woman."

Sampson sat back down again, across the table from Creed. "Glad I could help out. Hell, what are friends for?"

"Which is exactly why I showed up here," Creed said. "Not to roll with your woman, I don't mean. But for that other business I spoke to you about last night. You had time to think on that?"

Sampson pressed his coffee cup between his palms. "Not a whole lot to think on, really. Not for a pair of twenty-dollar gold pieces. That's how much you said, right?"

"You heard right." To emphasize the point, Creed patted a pocket of the too-small jacket he had on. A money pouch inside the pocket clinked enticingly. Creed had taken the jacket—along with the money pouch—off the body of a shopkeeper he'd killed night before last in a Denver back alley.

"For that much money, I'd ride to Hell and back," Sampson said.

"You don't have to go near that far. Like I told you," Creed reminded him, "you only have to hightail it up to the Pine Ridge rez and get word to Kicking Bear where he's holed up there with Sitting Bull. Tell him I'll have guns waiting for him in Vedauwoo. While you're doing that, I'll be making my way to get things ready for him."

"A hundred rifles, uh?"

"Springfield '73s. A little outdated, but brand new. Never fired. If Kicking Bear is serious about this Ghost Shirt stuff he's been preaching, he damn sure ought to be interested. Think how much hell he could stir up if all of a sudden if he was able to get his hands on that many guns."

"According to talk I've heard, I'd say you're right to think he'll be interested."

"Damn right I'm right."

Sampson looked thoughtful for a minute and then, somewhat cautiously, said, "If you don't mind me asking, Creed, what's in this for you? I mean, you don't generally do nothing for nothing. You ain't offering up those guns simply for the sake of helping this whole Indian reawakening thing get off the ground, are you?"

Creed looked at him like his question was the dumbest thing he'd ever heard. "Why the hell would I care if a bunch of stupid Indians dancing around in a circle ever 'reawake' anything, or not? Me and my mixed blood have been treated as bad by the Indians as by the whites. You know about that, too. I wouldn't lift a finger to help neither side if there wasn't something in it for me."

"So you *are* figuring to get some kind of payment out of Kicking Bear for those rifles."

"Damn right I am. Kicking Bear and me have had some dealings in the past. He don't like me much and he sure as hell don't claim me as kin. But he knows when I make a deal I stick to it. And I know he has ways to get his hands on money and gold still stashed away from the old Indian-raiding days. He wants these guns bad enough, he's gonna have to tap into some of that. You can tell him that for me. That'll be part of the message you carry to him."

29

"If you say so," Sampson allowed, not sounding wholly convinced.

"I say so," Creed growled irritably. "How about you let me worry whether or not Kicking Bear has the means to pay me? All you need to worry about is if I can pay *you* what we agreed on." He jerked the money pouch out of his jacket pocket, shook out a pair of twenty-dollar gold pieces, slapped them down on the rough-plank tabletop. "There! Now you got no worries for your part. You just make sure you do what you need to in order to earn that, then you can forget the rest."

Sampson said nothing. He held off touching the coins, but his eyes locked on them. He licked his lips like a hungry man gazing upon a feast. "When do you want me to ride out?" he asked.

"Right away. The sooner the better. You got a decent horse?"

"Uh-huh. Got a good one."

"You get started right away and stick to it hard and steady, you ought to make it to the rez by day after tomorrow. I'll have to take it a little slower and more careful on account of being on the dodge from every law dog this side of the Rockies. Still, that'd give me time to make it to Vedauwoo, find the guns and get them ready. Then figure two to four more days for Kicking Bear to reach me after you get word to him." Creed spread his hands. "So, no more than a week from now, the whole thing can be done. I take Kicking Bear's gold and make tracks for Canada, he takes the guns and goes off to finish stirring up his uprising or whatever the hell it's supposed to be. Everybody comes out happy."

Abruptly, Sampson reached for the coins on the table. "I know *I'm* going to come out happy," he said, smiling.

Creed's bearlike hand slammed down, pinning Sampson's wrist to the table, his fingers stopped an inch short of touching the gold pieces.

"Just to make sure we're clear," Creed said in a low, menacing tone. "I'm paying you in advance and counting on you to hold up your end. You fail me, Jack—for any reason, no excuses—it would displease me greatly. Understood?"

Sampson's smile had quickly given way to a pained expression as Creed's grip tightened on his wrist. "Yes," he groaned. "Jesus, Creed! Of course I understand."

Creed maintained his grip another agonizing minute. "See to it you do," he said, fierce black eyes emphasizing his message. Then, finally, he let go and Sampson pulled back his hand, feeling numbness in his arm all the way up to the shoulder.

4

"Man, oh man. That beats anything I ever did see," Milo Evert said in an awed, hushed voice. He continued looking through the long brass spyglass he was holding up to one eye. "Lookit him! That fella goes up and down and back and forth across those rocks like a doggone spider or something."

At Evert's right elbow, Flynn Remsen was also peering through a spyglass. His was aimed in the same general direction as Evert's, but at a lower level. "You go ahead and waste your time on that fool crawlin' around on the rocks if you want," muttered Remsen. "Me, I'd a whole lot rather stay tight on those two fine lookin' gals down there watchin' him—especially the blonde. Now *she* damn near beats anything I ever did see. Leastways not for a long, long while."

The two men were crouched in a stand of aspen on a slight rise above a weedy gully. On the other side of the gully, across a stretch of meadow grass, a high, flat-faced wall of granite cut with crooked fissures rose up well over a hundred feet. Part way up this natural wall, a man with a spool of rope draped over one shoulder and a string of what looked like sharp metal spikes dangling from his belt was making his way toward the top. He clung to hand-holds and found foot purchase in pinched cracks and on narrow ridges that seemed all but invisible to those watching.

At the base of the escarpment, necks craned back, anxious faces peering upward, two young women looked on. They were seated on a colorful picnic blanket that had been spread over the grass. A short distance off to one side of the women, a tall, slender man stood at a bulky camera mounted on a tripod, its lens tilted to capture the progress of the climber. Several yards removed from this group, seated on the dropped tailgate of a wagon hitched to a team of mules, a second man seemed to be keeping an eye on the overall proceedings.

In the aspen stand, Flynn Remsen lowered his spyglass and frowned. He was a homely, ill-kempt man in his middle thirties. He'd always been slight of build and frail-looking, the latter amplified even more in recent years by a bum left hip (the result of a bone-cracking bullet) that gave him a pronounced limp when he walked. He was clad in dirty, dusty trail clothes and a slouch hat that looked as if it had been in tug of war between two wolves. The pistol riding in a holster on his right hip and the Winchester rifle resting across his thigh, however, were glisteningly clean and well cared for.

"Elmer sent us to scout the area and hunt up some fresh meat," Remsen said now. "Reckon we've scouted up something—these rock-crawling fancies, I'm saying—we ought to report back to him about before we go shootin' off our guns at some game."

Evert nodded in agreement. In sharp contrast to Remsen, Evert was a tall, hard-muscled black man who moved with the grace of a mountain lion. He also wore rugged trail clothes, but his were kept brushed as clean as possible and the hat on his head was sharply creased and always cocked at just the right angle. The only visual similarity between the two men was the way they were both heavily armed and the obvious care they gave their guns.

"Yeah. I expect that'd be best," Evert drawled. "Don't see these fancies as much of a threat, but I'm pretty sure Elmer don't want to draw any undue attention to our bein' here."

Remsen grunted as he collapsed his spyglass and stuffed it in his coat pocket. With a final longing glance back across the meadow, he muttered, "Had my way, I'd damn well like to pay some attention to that fine-lookin' blonde over there. That's what *I'm* pretty sure of."

* * *

At the last sliver of morning, Cash came within sight of the familiar peaks and distinctive formations of the Vedauwoo rocks. By the middle of the afternoon, he'd reached the eastern fringe of the area and reined his horses to a halt beside a narrow stream running between banks of thick grass studded with various-sized rocks and boulders.

The day had warmed nicely, just a hint of breeze, and Cash had held a steady, distance-eating pace with only one prior stop to briefly rest and take on water. Now, having reached his destination, he felt warranted in allowing himself and the animals a lengthier break. After cooling the horses, he watered them at the stream and then staked them to forage in the rich grass while he set some coffee to brew over a small, smokeless fire and opened a can of peaches to eat along with strips of beef jerky. Once the coffee was ready, he poured himself a cup and stretched out in a patch of shade, resting on hip and elbow, to enjoy his repast.

In that relaxed moment, Cash's thoughts once again drifted to the visits he'd made here as a boy, often coming to this very stream. He lingered in the reverie for only a short time, however, before pulling his thoughts to the present and to the task that had returned him here.

Cash had his doubts that Creed was already in the vicinity, yet he'd have to proceed with caution just in case. More likely, the ruthless fugitive was still making his way here, along the way gathering necessary provisions and possibly one or two additional men for assistance. In any event, Cash's plan for finding him once he *was* present in the area remained unchanged.

His intent was to work his way deeper into Vedauwoo, establish a well-concealed base camp, and then begin a vigil for the purpose of spotting Creed as soon as he poked up his evil head. This vigil, he'd decided, would be conducted primarily from a high point on one of the central mounds referred to by the Arapaho as the Turtle. Cash knew a relatively easy route to the top of the Turtle and from there he would have a good view over most of Vedauwoo, able to look down on all but the higher peaks of a few other mounds.

A glimpse of movement, a flicker of light in the darkness, a wisp of campfire smoke … it was by means such as these that Cash was counting on Creed to reveal himself. And when he did, Cash would be ready to respond.

* * *

William Hattner lightly dropped the final six feet to the ground. A few beads of sweat dotted his forehead, but otherwise there was no outward evidence of the exertion that had been necessary to make the climb and descent he'd just completed. He was scarcely even breathing hard. William was a tall, solidly trim young man of twenty-five and when he turned away from the granite cliff to face the others as they approached, his handsome face beamed with a bright, confident smile.

Abandoning the camera and tripod with which he'd recorded some spectacular shots of his cousin's rock climbing prowess, Jonathan Kelsey was the first to reach William. He clasped the climber's hand and pumped it eagerly, all the while wearing his own broad smile. Jonathan was a year younger than William, equally tall, skinnier and a bit gawkier in physical stature, but also quite handsome in a somewhat more boyish way.

"That was amazing! Absolutely incredible!" Jonathan fairly gushed. "I never saw anything like it—although I shouldn't be surprised that such feats of daring would be something you would pursue, cousin."

"Feats of madness, would be more like it," suggested dark-haired Alice Amberson, one of the two young women who'd been looking on from the nearby picnic blanket. The pair had risen and started over together, with Alice advancing anxiously ahead of her close friend, Melanie Parsons. Both were in their early twenties and both quite attractive, though in quite opposite ways—Alice dark and sultry; Melanie a fair-skinned, coolly challenging ice goddess.

"My heart leapt into my throat a half dozen times as you clung so precariously to the tiniest slivers of rock," Alice continued. "All I could think of was why I'd ever agreed to such reckless insanity less than a week ahead of the grand wedding we've been planning for so long."

Hattner chuckled. "Was it my safety you were concerned for, dear Alice, or the strain it might put on your precious wedding if the best man so rudely chose the last minute to inconveniently slip and break his bloody fool neck?"

"Really, William," Alice sniffed as she moved to Jonathan's side, pressing close and slipping her arm through his. "As the cousin and best friend of my betrothed, concern that no harm befell you was all I meant to express—wedding notwithstanding."

"Wishing no harm goes without saying," spoke up Melanie Parsons. "Otherwise, I for one found the whole thing very exciting, Mr. Hattner."

William conjured a fresh smile especially for her. "I am pleased you enjoyed it, Miss Parsons."

"What's more," Jonathan interjected, "if the photographs I just took turn out even a fraction as good as I believe they will, I predict we can generate similar excitement in others. Surely I will be able to place some of these shots in one or more of the Denver newspapers—and no doubt an article or interview to go with them. With that kind of exposure, it's inconceivable to me that this sport William has brought over from abroad—this *rock climbing*, as he calls it—won't catch on and become wildly popular with other adventurous souls right here in the States."

"You might be surprised," William cautioned. "I was there when Haskett-Smith made his widely heralded climb of the Naples Needle at Great Gable. While that certainly got a good deal of newspaper attention, the popularity of rock climbing as a sport still hasn't managed to gain much in the way of wide popularity, at least not in Europe."

"But with the Rocky Mountains right on Denver's back doorstep," said Melanie, "if it's going to catch on anywhere, I should think there could hardly be a more ideal spot."

William shrugged. "Perhaps. No doubt the Rockies are already a world-renowned magnet for mountain climbers. And I'm sure there are cliffs and walls there that would be equally suited to rock climbing. Nevertheless, the two activities are actually quite exclusive to one another. But *this* place," he swept his arms, indicating the sprawl of Vedawoo, "with its countless high, sheer walls and magnificent fissures and peaks, it's like the Creator *made* it for rock climbing. That was why, after I saw the photos hanging on the wall of Jonathan's office from his previous trip here, I pleaded to make this visit."

"I highly doubt," Alice said in a rather imperious tone, "that God was concerned with the different ways His reckless little humans might find to risk breaking their bloody fool necks—as you so quaintly put it, William— when he created the mighty Rockies, let alone this leftover pile of sun-blasted rubble."

"Be that as it may," William responded, "He did a spectacular job here all the same. Spectacular enough that I dare say I would very much like to try my luck on a couple more pieces of His rubble before we depart."

Alice looked aghast. "Oh no! We cannot afford to tarry here a moment longer than planned. We must get back and put the finishing touches on my wedding arrangements. We must leave first thing in the morning. Even at that, with a two-day return trip to Denver, we will be cutting it uncomfortably close."

Patting the leather harness around his waist and the spool of rope draped over one shoulder, William said, "While I'm all rigged up for it, I can fit in another climb yet today before the light fades. Then all I'm asking is for a few more hours tomorrow—half the morning, at most—to scale that magnificent escarpment more toward the interior there." He pointed to a towering granite outcropping with a weather-worn face. "I'm begging everyone's indulgence. Please, Jonathan, think of the fantastic shots and the shadow contrasts you'll be able to get with the morning sun flowing down on that wall as I make my way up."

Jonathan looked simultaneously intrigued by the prospect yet highly uncomfortable over the dilemma it presented. It was clear he would welcome the photographic opportunity— *if* it didn't pose such a direct conflict with the wishes of his bride-to-be, who stood glaring at his side, her eyes demanding to hear his decision.

Fortunately, the appearance of Leonard Cory, the wagon driver and guide who had led the party from Denver, provided a timely and most welcome interruption. Striding up from where he'd been waiting and watching at the wagon, he drawled, "You folks decided yet on where you want to pitch night camp? I oughta get the mules unhitched and start settin' things up, if you have. Ain't a bad spot right here, you ask me. Level ground, grass for the mules, nice little pond right over yonder. Your call to make, but we're gonna start losin' the light 'fore long in case you want to move somewheres else."

* * *

"Wait a minute." A hard frown tugged on Elmer Post's haggard, heavily stubbled face. "You tellin' me there's some idiot out there climbin' up and down these rugged cliffs for no reason other than just to be *doin'* it? He ain't even climbin' *after* something or to get *away* from something?"

Flynn Remsen nodded firmly. "That's the way of it. We seen it with our own eyes."

"For a fact," Milo Evert confirmed. "We watched for a good spell and that's what he was up to, nothing else but."

"Why the hell didn't Danton spot him and come report it?" Elmer wanted to know.

"This fella we're talkin' about is way over on the south fringe, other side of some of those high rocks that shoot practically straight up," Remsen replied. "No way to spot him from our lookout post."

Elmer seemed to grudgingly accept the explanation and stood silent for a minute, pondering this new development. He was a tall, lean, ruggedly built man with a hard glint to his eyes and a square jaw that seemed permanently clenched in a way that always gave him a grim expression.

The discussion was taking place in a secluded, cavern-like notch formed naturally within a jumble of tall, broken boulders overhung with aspen growth and crowded with ground level evergreen bushes. The ashes of a cold campfire were spread near the mouth of the notch. A short distance away, in another stand of aspen and good grass, five horses stood quietly hobbled.

"Climbin' rocks just for the hell of it," Elmer finally grunted. "Craziest damn thing I ever heard. And he's got others with him, you say? You sure they ain't caretakers from some loony bin sneakin' around to try and drop a net

41

over him so's they can haul him back and lock him up where he rightfully belongs?"

Evert shook his head. "Near as we could tell, they was on hand sort of for support. Cheering him on, taking pictures and so forth."

"Takin' pictures?"

"Uh-huh. Got one of those big old boxy cameras on stilts. Real professional looking. The fella doing the climbing looked sort of professional, too, come to think on it. Had some kind of leather harness around his waist for hooking up to the coil of rope he had over his shoulder. Had little metal spikes, too, that he drove in where he didn't have nothing else to grab hold of. Mostly, though, he managed to find footholds and handholds at the doggonedest places right in the rock itself."

Elmer pursed his lips thoughtfully. "Seems pretty clear he came here *meanin'* to do some rock climbin'. Came prepared."

"Oh, he came prepared all right," said Remsen with a nasty chuckle. "He even brought along those two women to help handle the chilly nights that will be settin' in."

"Never mind the damn women," Elmer snapped. "Far as that goes, never mind the whole bunch of 'em. Sounds to me like they're nothing more than a fancified picnic party. I don't see how that makes 'em much of a threat to us."

"One way to make certain they ain't no threat to us," Remsen suggested.

Evert shot him a glance that made it clear he didn't like that idea at all.

Elmer made it clear he felt the same, saying, "Now how smart of an idea is that, Flynn? How long you figure it'd be before somebody back wherever this bunch came from would miss 'em and come a-lookin'? Then where would that leave us? We'd have a whole passel of folks—with law dogs most likely in the mix—crawlin' all over this place."

"Maybe we'd be gone before anybody like that showed up."

"Yeah, and maybe we wouldn't be, either. You see how bad Virgil's hurt." Elmer jerked his head toward a still form that lay deeper in the recess of the notch, wrapped in saddle blankets lying on a bed of pine boughs. Some of the blankets had been torn into strips for bandages, soaked through with blood that had dried to blackish stains. "It's gonna take a while to get him healed strong enough to ride. We can hole up right here and take all the time he needs. Long as we don't do something dumb that causes us to get flushed out ahead of then."

Remsen squinted. "I don't hold much for bein' called dumb, Elmer. Not even from you."

"Then don't come up with dumb ideas," Elmer replied flatly, "and there won't be any problem."

The two locked flinty gazes for a long count, then Remsen looked off. "Okay. Before we gave ourselves away to those picnickers by takin' a shot at some critter, we thought it best to check with you. Was that a dumb idea, too?"

"No, it wasn't," Elmer replied, most the edge slipping from his voice. "I appreciate the consideration. But, judgin' from the way you've described that rock climber and his friends, if they hear shootin' they sound like the kind more apt to run *away* from it than toward it."

Evert nodded. "Most likely. The climber and the picture-taker looked like a couple of dandies, that's for sure. The only one who appeared to maybe have any bark on him at all was the older fella tending the mules and driving the wagon. No towns or settlements anywhere close, so the dandies must've traveled a distance to get here and probably hired the older fella to drive them out."

"Hired help," Elmer said disdainfully. "That means he likely ain't got enough stake in their little picnic to stick out his neck for 'em."

"Safe bet," Evert agreed.

"All right, then. You boys go ahead back out and bag us some meat for supper, you hear? Don't get too carried away with your blastin' though. No sense drawin' any more attention to us than need be. But do what you have to."

After Remsen and Evert had departed again, Elmer turned and walked back to kneel beside the wounded man on the pine boughs. He gently placed the back of his hand on the victim's forehead, feeling for any sign of fever. There was none. If anything, the pale flesh of the forehead felt too cool. Elmer moved his hand to the wounded man's chest and rested it there lightly. The rise and fall of breathing was shallow, but steady.

Elmer rocked back on his heels and gazed down on the wounded man. Little more than a boy, really, the clean lines of his face unravaged by years and scarcely capable of growing beard bristle. The resemblance to Elmer's own face was there if one looked closely enough, but it had been a long time since Elmer's craggy visage had appeared that fresh and young.

"You hang in there, baby brother. You hear me?" Elmer said softly, huskily. "You hang tough, the way us Posts always do. I'll let you rest as long as you need to build your strength back up. We're safe here. The bleedin' is stopped and I got some fresh meat comin'. You just rest and keep gettin' stronger, that's your job. Soon as you're up to it, we'll head back home to Oklahoma, just like I promised."

If Virgil Post heard any of these words, he gave no response.

Elmer squatted there for a long time, just gazing down at his younger brother, knowing he was clinging to life only by a thread. Elmer had never learned how to pray and he told himself it was too late to start now, but a part of him wished that it wasn't.

5

Cash had just reached the top of the Turtle when the rifle report rang out—a single, sharp crack of sound cutting through the surrounding stillness of Vedauwoo. It caused the marshal to drop reflexively into a low crouch and duck for cover behind a weather-flattened boulder. A fraction of a second later, however, even as he settled to one knee behind the boulder, Cash came to the realization that the shot hadn't been meant for him. If it had, judging by the distant, rolling boom of the discharge, he knew the bullet would have struck or whined somewhere close before the sound of the shot ever reached his ears.

Yet, while there was some consolation in recognizing that no one seemed to be shooting directly *at* him, the fact there was gunfire taking place at all was still reason enough for caution.

With his Winchester clutched to his chest, Cash bellied over to the rim of the mound and scanned slow and careful to the north, the direction from which the shot seemed to have originated. Given the rugged terrain of mounds and ridges cut with twisting trails and gullies and shallow canyons, he was well aware that sound could bounce in funny ways here. Still, he was reasonably convinced that— yes, there it was! Movement on the far edge of a teardrop-shaped clearing, a meadow of short grass starting to turn brown this late in the season. Two men brandishing rifles had just hurried across the neck of the clearing and now stopped to hover over a brownish object barely discernable in the grass a few feet short of the tree line that marked the northwest boundary of the clearing. As Cash watched, the two men set aside their rifles and dropped to their knees beside the object in the grass.

Laying aside his own Winchester, Cash withdrew from the leather case dangling at his chest a pair of binoculars. He raised these to his eyes and adjusted the lenses for a closer look. He quickly saw that the object in the grass was a freshly slain mule deer and the two men were beginning to field dress it. Both men were dressed in rugged trail clothes, one a bit shabbier-looking than the other. Each man wore a gun belt and holstered pistol on his hip. The shabby looking one was slight in build and favored a limp on his left side, the other was a strapping black man with a crisp hat perched almost jauntily atop his head.

Hunters. Bagging fresh meat. Perhaps to eat immediately, perhaps to cure and store for the upcoming winter.

Cash continued to watch as the pair went about their business, knives flashing, blood flowing. They clearly knew what they were doing and appeared to have teamed for this sort of thing before.

Hunters.

Up until now, Cash's concentration had strictly been on encountering Vilo Creed in this place; plus maybe a couple of cohorts if he managed to attract any followers on his way here. What he hadn't reckoned on was running into anybody else in Vedauwoo. Which, when he stopped to think about it, had been decidedly short-sighted. After all, hunters like the Arapaho tribe of his boyhood had been coming to stalk the rich variety of game to be found here for as long as anyone knew. And now that the Indians had all been corralled onto reservations, it should come as no surprise that white men—or, in this case, a white man and a black man—might come around for the same reason.

Cash frowned. The presence of hunters, in and of itself, was of no particular concern to him. What *was* cause for concern, though, was the question of how long they figured on sticking around. Hell, for that matter, what if there were *more* hunters in the area? The last thing Cash wanted was to have unsuspecting innocents on hand and thereby at risk when Creed showed up.

There was nothing else for it, Cash decided sourly, but to go down there and warn those two fools what was afoot and then chase them the hell away ... along with anybody else who might be in the vicinity, if that turned out to be the case.

As these thoughts ran through his mind, Cash continued to keep his field glasses trained on the two men down in the clearing. The strapping black was a stranger, of that much he was certain. But there was something familiar about the other man. He was working with his head lowered, so Cash caught only brief glimpses of his face. Still, it was enough to trigger some niggling sense that he ought to recognize those features. *Small man ... lame ... shabby dresser ... pinched, homely face ...*

And then, abruptly, Cash had it.

Flynn Remsen.

Flynn Remsen, originally from down Kansas way. Rustler, back shooter, highwayman, train robber, and

49

general all around no-good hombre. Reported to have been riding with Elmer Post's gang over in Nebraska for the past two or three years, specializing in hitting trains carrying large sums of money sent from big eastern banks to branch operations sprouting on the Western frontier.

Damn. That made Remsen something different from just a simple hunter. He might be hunting at the moment, but Cash was willing to bet he was up to something more than that. Something no good, if past history meant anything.

A wild thought crossed Cash's mind: Could it be that Remsen was here to meet up with Creed? Could it be their lawless paths had crossed at some previous point and now Creed had somehow sent word ahead for Remsen—hell, maybe the whole Post gang, for that matter—to join him in his scheme involving the stolen guns? Or maybe they'd already joined up and Creed was already here too, in spite of what Cash had convinced himself earlier. Any of these possibilities seemed improbable to the point of being mighty tough to swallow. But having two or more high profile outlaws turn up at exactly the same time at exactly the same remote location was stretching the bounds of coincidence to the point of also being hard to swallow.

Cash lowered the field glasses and swore under his breath. No matter what, his immediate course of action remained the same. He had to go down there. Only now it would be to do more than warn off a couple of "hunters" who showed up in the wrong place at the wrong time—now he needed to find out what the hell *else* it was they were up to.

* * *

Jonathan Kelsey straightened up abruptly from peering through his camera. He took a step back and swung his gaze in a hundred and eighty degree sweep. "What was that?" he said.

From where he was setting up a pair of large tents nearby, Leonard Cory glanced up also and said, "Rifle shot."

Alice Amberson and Melanie Parsons sat sipping tea at a foldout table half way between where Jonathan had his camera positioned and where Cory was erecting the tents. With her teacup raised part way to her lips, Alice's eyes went suddenly wide. "A rifle shot?" she echoed. "My goodness, are we in danger?"

On the edge of the clearing where the others were gathered, fifty feet in the air, dangling precariously from a granite cliff face, William Hattner twisted his face and shoulders to look down at them. "By the sound of it," he called, "it came from a good distance away. Off to the north. You needn't fear, Alice, no one is shooting at us."

"Hunters bagging some fresh meat," Cory amended. "Nothing for us to be concerned about."

"It's quite common for this area, dear," Jonathan said to his fiancé. "My first visit to Vedauwoo—the trip that allowed me to get those initial photographs that so impressed William—was with a party of hunters. We really have no reason to be alarmed."

"No reason as long as they're careful about which way they aim their loud old nasty guns," Alice insisted. "A stray bullet can be just as deadly as a purposefully aimed one, can it not?"

"No worries, Alice. They're too far away," floated down William's voice. "Besides, no bullet can twist and turn its way through all the boulders and mounds between us and where they're shooting from." Craning her shapely neck to peer up at the climber, Melanie flashed a teasing smile and said, "That may be true for those of us down here on the ground—but what about you, scampering around up there like a giant fly on a slice of angel food cake? What if they can see you from wherever they're at and decide you might make something interesting to have stuffed and mounted in their trophy room?"

William grinned down at her. "That's not even funny."

"No, it's not," said Alice stiffly. "Not funny at all."

Cory shrugged. "Either way, ain't nothing to get in a tizzy over. Just hunters huntin'. No reason to think they even know we're here."

* * *

Cash had little trouble finding the spot where Flynn Remsen and the black stranger had field-dressed their deer. From there it was easy enough to cut sign for the route the pair had subsequently taken. It wasn't surprising that they made no effort to hide their tracks; they had no reason to think it necessary.

Dusk was descending now, the sun only a fading glow behind Vedauwoo's western peaks. Cash moved along cautiously but briskly. He had little doubt he could find his way back to his own camp by the light of the moon and stars, but not even he was a good enough tracker to follow ground sign if it got too dark.

He'd covered little more than a half mile from the deer kill site, however, when he smelled smoke from a fresh fire and the unmistakable aroma of coffee cooking. He slowed his pace and stayed to the shadows cast by surrounding aspen and fir as he continued to edge forward. When the trees gave way to a sprawl of rock and rubble spilled away from the base of one of the sharply rising escarpments found so frequently within Vedauwoo, he could see a handful of men hunched over a small fire at the mouth of a ragged notch cut back into a pile of massive boulders.

Cash eased up as close as he dared, then dropped to his right knee with his Winchester resting across his left thigh. There were three men gathered around the fire. Two of them were Flynn Remsen and the black stranger Cash had seen earlier through his field glasses. The third was none other than Elmer Post, leader of the gang Remsen was known to have been riding with in recent years.

The men were talking in low voices as they cut up generous slices of the venison and hung them on a spit over the fire.

"We ain't gonna go hungry while we're holed up here, that much is for sure," the black man was saying. "All kinds of game out there, just waiting to be taken. And I bet there's plenty of fish in some of these streams and ponds, too."

"Why do you think I steered us here?" Elmer replied. "Once we'd set a false trail leadin' that stupid damn posse back toward Nebraska, I knew there wasn't no better place to head for."

Remsen stabbed at a piece of meat with an aggression that indicated he wasn't feeling anywhere near as content as his two companions. "Well, I'm real glad you two are so tickled over bein' hunkered down in a pile of rocks gnawin' on wild game and a bunch of bony fish," he grumbled. "Me, I had this silly notion that with my cut of the money we

53

hauled off the Omaha Flyer the other night I'd be livin' a helluva lot higher on the hog than this."

"Jesus, don't you ever get sick of bellyachin'?" Elmer wanted to know.

"When I do, you'll be the first to know. And you know when that'll be? When we get somewhere where I can start spendin' free and livin' high, that's when."

"The money, including your cut, ain't going nowhere," the black man pointed out. "When the time is right for us to ride out of here, it'll still spend just fine."

"Yeah, and it'd spend just as goddamn fine right now, too—the sooner the better, says I."

"Awright, that's enough," Elmer barked irritably. "It's already settled. Nobody's goin' nowhere to spend nothin' until Virgil is healed enough to ride. Then we'll split the take from that train job and go our separate ways. Me'n Virg will be headed back to Oklahoma, the rest of you can aim where you please. In the meantime, nobody's cuttin' out on their own to run the risk of gettin' caught by that posse and leadin' 'em back here while my brother ain't strong enough to have any chance of ridin' clear."

Remsen thrust out his chin defiantly. "How long we been ridin' together, Elmer? You don't know me well enough by now to know there ain't no chance in hell I'd ever spill to any damn posse and lead 'em back to you? That's a hell of a thing to say to me!"

"It's true we've been together a long time, Flynn. And I trust you like blood kin," Elmer allowed. "But I got my mind made up on this. We don't scatter from here until we're all able to scatter together."

Remsen muttered something in response, only Cash couldn't make out what it was.

But he'd already heard enough to have his mind racing. They'd mentioned robbing a train, the Omaha Flyer. Cash recalled Chief Penn saying something back in Cheyenne about having men out investigating a train robbery. That had to be this bunch—the Elmer Post gang. And now, while a posse presumably including one or more of Cash's fellow marshals was off chasing an alleged "false trail," here he was with the robbers all of a sudden practically in his lap!

Under different circumstances, he might welcome this ironic turn of events. Might even consider it a stroke of luck. Never one to lack self-confidence, Cash figured that, with the element of surprise working in his favor, he could manage to get the drop on these owlhoots and have them in irons before full dark. If he wanted to. Only there was where a dilemma entered in. If he saddled himself with taking these three—make that four, counting the wounded "Virgil," who apparently was laid up farther back in the cave-like notch— into custody, where would that leave him as far as being able to intercept and stop Vilo Creed if and when he showed up?

Cash swore under his breath.

The only good thing about this predicament, he told himself, was that he didn't have to decide right then and there how he wanted to handle it. From what he'd overheard, it didn't sound like Elmer or his men would be going anywhere any time soon. On the other hand, he could hardly afford to ignore them—not for very long. With Creed expected to make an appearance in the next day or so, the last thing Cash needed was for the Post Gang to still be on the loose and in the same vicinity when it came time for him to try and apprehend the fugitive half breed. There was little doubt whose side Elmer and his pack would take if they caught wind of *anybody* going up against a lawman.

Cash pondered a minute longer. He'd just about made up his mind to return to his own camp and chew things a little finer there. But then, from only a foot or so directly behind him, the unmistakable click of a revolver being cocked froze him exactly as he was.

"I don't know who the hell you are, mister. But I double-damn sure know you don't belong here," grumbled a low voice from right about where the hammer-cock had sounded. "Get those hands in the air and follow 'em up. On your feet, real slow. Let the rifle drop. Make even one wrong twitch, I'll blow your head into the middle of tomorrow."

Cash did as he was told. Straightened up slow and careful, let his Winchester slip to the ground.

"Danton, is that you?" somebody called from the camp. "What the hell's goin' on out there?"

"Keep a sharp eye peeled, Elmer," responded the man behind Cash. "Caught somebody skulkin' the camp. Might be more. I got the drop on this one, I'm gonna bring him—"

In that instant—that split second while the man behind him was overly confident he had everything under control and his attention was momentarily diverted by the exchange with Elmer—Cash sensed he had the best chance he was likely to get for trying to escape this predicament. If he waited until he was led into the camp, where he would be under the muzzles of four guns instead of just one, the odds against him would multiply accordingly and after they spotted his badge they might simply shoot him down like a dog, no further questions asked.

Making this decision, he abruptly collapsed at the knees and dropped into a low crouch—low enough so that he hoped he had ducked under the pistol allegedly aimed at the back of his head. At the same time he pitched backward with his torso and shoulders, slamming his upper body into that of the man breathing down his neck, kicking his legs straight again and driving his full weight as hard as he could into chest, ribs, and a spongy stomach. His target emitted a loud grunt and a *whumpf!* of sour-smelling breath as he staggered backward under the impact. The pistol he'd been aiming— arm now draped over Cash's shoulder, gun hand extended out away from his face—discharged with a fierce roar. As the shooter's feet became entangled and he started to topple to the ground, dragging Cash with him, Cash grabbed the arm braced over his shoulder and wrenched savagely downward, forcing the arm to bend in a way it never was meant to bend. The elbow socket popped and cracked like a dry tree branch being busted up for kindling and its owner screamed in agony.

Cash and the shooter—Danton, Elmer Post had called him—hit the ground hard, Cash's weight again slamming the man who only seconds ago had him under the gun. The marshal arced his back, grinding down a moment longer on Danton, now pinned under him. Then he snapped forward to a sitting position, pausing only long enough to slash viciously backward with each of his elbows, using them to batter either side of Danton's head.

Springing to his feet, Cash drew his own Colt with his right hand and also took time to reach down with his left and snatch up the pistol that had fallen from the other man's grip when Cash broke his arm. He couldn't see where his

Winchester had ended up and he couldn't afford time to hunt for it.

In the robbers' camp, the men there were all on their feet, scrambling excitedly and bringing into view a menacing array of guns.

"Danton! Danton! What the hell is goin' on out there?" Elmer Post demanded.

"Take cover, Elmer," Danton responded in an agonized groan. "The bastard got the better of me!"

"You heard the man," Cash snarled as he planted his feet wide and took a stance in the murkiness behind the tree line. "Duck for cover, you sonsabitches!"

With a pistol in each hand, Cash opened up on the camp, pouring in a rapid-fire barrage that kicked up dust and campfire sparks and whined off rocks like a symphony of sizzling lead. If Elmer and the others had been scrambling excitedly before, now they were sent into a leaping, diving frenzy that was almost comical as they sought to gain some kind of cover amidst the boulders and broken rubble. A moment later, however, when they rose back up brandishing their weapons and taking wild aim, there was nothing funny about the hail of hot lead they sent blazing back as return fire. Bullets sang through the air high and low, slapping through tree leaves, splattering underbrush.

But by then Cash had already wheeled about and was beating a retreat, streaking away through the deepening shadows of descending dusk. Before he dissolved from sight entirely, though, one stubborn slug managed to catch up with him and cut a burning furrow about six inches under his right armpit. The punch of the bullet staggered him for two or three steps but he continued running and a moment later there was no sign of him.

In his wake, he could hear Danton wailing, "Elmer! Fellas! Jesus Christ, don't forget I'm still out here, too—Watch where you're shootin', dammit!"

6

On the south side of Vedauwoo, five people stood in uneasy silence. All were cast partly in the soft shadows of arriving dusk and partly in the flickering gold-orange glow thrown by the large campfire around which they were gathered. All were gazing off to the north, faces set in expressions of concern, eyes shining anxiously.

It was Jonathan Kelsey who broke the silence, saying, "I'm hardly a wilderness veteran, but all that shooting—it sure didn't sound like hunters to me."

"Wasn't," responded Leonard Cory tersely, the lines in his leathery old face deepened by a hard frown.

"What was it then?" Jonathan wanted to know.

"Can't say for certain, but it sounded more like a gunfight of some kind."

"That's exactly what it sounded like," agreed William Hattner.

Alice Amberson looked startled. "You mean, as in men *shooting at one another*?"

"That's the way it usually works," said William.

"But a gunfight clear out here in the middle of nowhere?" Melanie Parsons gave a faint shake of her pretty blonde head. "What could be the reason for something like that?"

Cory grunted. "Some men don't need a whole lot of reason to start throwin' lead back and forth." His eyes were scanning edgily. "If that shot we heard earlier came from somebody in a hunting party, then maybe some members of the party got into a disagreement, had a falling out over something. Maybe liquor involved. Maybe a pack of lawmen or bounty hunters ran an owlhoot to ground up there—wouldn't be the first time an outlaw on the dodge tried to lose himself in Vedauwoo until the heat cooled off him."

"It couldn't be Indians, could it?" blurted Alice, her voice trembling.

"The Indians are all on reservations, dear," Jonathan told her soothingly. "Besides, if it were Indians, there wouldn't have been near as much shooting. They strike silently. Bows and arrows, remember?"

Cory gave the pair of soon-to-be-weds a pitying look. "Just for the record," he said, "even though I don't figure that's what's going on—Indians *have* been known to jump their reservations. And they've also been known to find ways of getting their hands on guns and learning to use them right smart."

"Oh my God!" Alice wailed.

Jonathan scowled at Cory. "That was a cruel and unnecessary thing for you to say, sir."

Cory spread his hands. "Just tellin' it straight, that's all."

"It seems to me," interjected William, "that the main question we need to address is whether or not those shots—whatever their origin or cause—present any potential threat to us."

"The simplest and safest answer to that," Cory replied, "is to go ahead and reckon they do—or at least *might*. That means we ought to take some basic precautions, starting by not advertising our presence here anymore than need be. We should douse our fire and run a cold camp for the balance of the night. Forget the tents, too. Best if we stick together, sort of forted up. Suggest you bring your sleeping gear from the tents and we all bunch up around the wagon, with somebody standing guard through 'til morning."

William nodded. "That all sounds reasonable to me. I say we do exactly as Mr. Cory suggests."

Alice bristled immediately and visibly. "No fire? No hot food? The lot of us crammed together in a sleeping arrangement not unlike a—a *Roman orgy*? I should say not! I will remind one and all that I am a lady."

"What is that supposed to mean—that I'm *not*?" demanded Melanie.

Alice met her fiery glare. "I don't hear you protesting against such outlandish proposals."

"I'm not protesting because they make good sense."

"Ladies, ladies—please." Jonathan held up his hands and tried to insert himself between the two women. "Remember you are the best of friends. Compose yourselves before you say something you will both regret."

"Shut up, Jonathan!" Alice and Melanie shouted in unison.

"I suggest all three of you take that advice," William said offhandedly, as he joined Cory in starting to kick dirt and gravel over the campfire, smothering the flames. "Put aside your thoughts of personal comfort and prissy proprieties—you, Alice, especially and start thinking about what you can do for our overall good. You can begin by striking those tents and bringing the sleeping blankets over to spread under the wagon, exactly as Mr. Cory instructed."

Jonathan stiffened. "I don't think I care for your tone, William. Particularly not directed toward my fiancé in such a manner."

"We can take up your displeasure with my rudeness another time, Jonathan," replied William as he continued to help kill the fire. "In the meantime, if you truly wish to show some spine and make noises like a man, then you'd be well advised to start by standing up to the love of your life and getting her to do something constructive for a change—or, at the very least, cease her endless whining and complaining."

* * *

In the train robbers' camp, a considerable amount of discord was also taking place.

In addition to breaking James Danton's arm, Cash had caused further damage to the Post Gang when one of the bullets from his double-barreled barrage ricocheted straight into the scrawny left thigh of Flynn Remsen, shattering the main bone there. Since this was the leg already affected by the damaged hip from a previous bullet wound, this new injury left the victim not only in great pain but it diminished his mobility to practically nothing.

"That dirty, miserable sonofabitch," Remsen was lamenting from where he leaned back on a flat boulder near the crackling campfire, his freshly bandaged and splinted leg propped up on a saddle. "Why did it have to be me he shot? I was already half-crippled, why did he have to go and make it worse? Everything bad always happens to me!"

"You think this busted arm is a picnic?" Danton said through gritted teeth. He was a bearish man with massive shoulders and bulging jowls under a thick, curly beard. "You ain't the only one who caught some bad luck here this evening, Flynn, so quit carrying on like you are."

"Yeah, and we all know who we can thank for every bit of it, don't we?" Remsen snapped back. "You had the sonofabitch right under your gun. What'd you do—take time to scratch your nuts so he had the chance to turn tables on you?"

"Knock it off, the both of you!" barked Elmer, back-handing away some of the grease smearing the heavy stubble on his chin and around his mouth from the piece of venison he was eating. "That kind of bickerin' ain't gonna gain us a damn thing, so put a boot in it … I need time to think."

"What's to think about?" Remsen wanted to know. "One of them rock-climbin' dandies was spyin' on us and fumble-footed Danton here—who was supposed to be on lookout and never should have let anybody get that close in the first place—managed to trip over him on the way back to camp, spookin' our visitor into blastin' hell out of everything in sight. Oh yeah, and while he was at it he *loaned* him one of the guns to do his blastin' with."

Danton's face purpled. "How about I fumble-foot my way over there and kick your bony ass all the way to—"

Now Elmer's bark turned into a roar. "Goddamn it, that's enough! I said knock it off!"

"You need to listen to the man," said Milo Evert, speaking around a bite of venison he'd just taken, "if for no other reason than for the sake of your wounds. Look what you gone and done already." He pointed to fresh blood

65

leaking through the bandage on Remsen's thigh. "I just got that patched up and now you've opened it again, getting yourself so agitated. I think I got most of the bullet fragments out but I don't have the skill to dig around any deeper, even if I didn't. Main thing is: It don't need no added aggravation. Same goes for you," he added, cutting his gaze to Danton, whose damaged arm was immobilized and bound tight to his torso by strips of well-worn saddle blanket. "At best, you're both gonna be in a whole lot of pain and bother. Ain't that enough?"

"Don't worry about me, I know how to handle pain," Remsen muttered, his tone subdued though still sullen. "The only pain I'm thinkin' about right now is the pain I'm gonna lay down on that sonofabitch who shot me." His eyes narrowed dangerously. "We *are* going after those bastards, ain't we, Elmer?"

The gang leader nodded solemnly. "Got no choice."

"Now you're talkin'," said Remsen. "You had me a little worried—when I mentioned goin' after 'em before you was dead set against it. Said we couldn't risk the search party that'd come to look for 'em if they didn't make it back."

"That was before. Back when I figured they'd take no interest in us and therefore pose no threat. Now that one of 'em has shown otherwise, we can hardly leave 'em to go blabbin' back wherever they came from, can we? Plus, they've blooded us—no sonofabitch walks away from that without gettin' payback. And as far as any search party that might come around … well, we'll have to deal with that if and when the time comes."

"Now you're talkin'," Remsen said again, biting aggressively into his own piece of venison and tearing off a huge bite.

It was broodingly quiet for a moment, until Evert said, "Thing I can't help wondering, though, is if our visitor from a little while ago actually was part of that rock climbing bunch."

The others all looked at him.

"Who the hell else would it be?" Elmer demanded. "Ain't nobody else around here."

"Can we be sure of that? We didn't know those rock climbers existed, either, until only a little while ago."

"I was up on that lookout roost all damn day," Danton argued. "I didn't see no sign of anybody."

"Including the skulker who ended up shooting at us— not until you came upon him when you was returning to camp." Evert quickly raised his hands in a defensive gesture. "And I don't mean that you should have or even *could* have spotted him before then. That's my whole point. With all the mounds and hills and trees and gullies around here, you could march a couple cavalry patrols in and out and— depending where you happened to be located—never notice hide nor hair of them."

"That may be," Elmer said, scowling. "But then the point becomes: How many folks you figure come traipsin' through here at any given time? You figure this is the goddamn Deadwood stage depot or something?"

Evert shook his head. "I have no idea how many people are apt to pass this way. Yes, I realize it's a remote spot. All I'm saying is that there's *room* for several groups of people to be here at the same time and not necessarily bump into one another. Plus, I keep thinking back to the impression Flynn and me both got from those rock climbers. The actions of whoever it was who shot at us tonight … well, doggone it, it just don't *fit* with the kind of people we saw there."

"He's kinda got a point, Elmer," said Remsen, licking his fingers loudly and then scrunching up his face in consideration. "They weren't nothin' but a bunch of dandies, just like we told you. Hard to believe one of them could've got the drop on Danton and then had the skill or the gumption, either one, to start blazin' away like he done."

"You said they had a wagon driver with 'em, didn't you? Said he looked to have some bark on him. Right?"

"*Some* bark, yeah," Remsen allowed. "But he also looked to have quite a few years on him. Can't picture him lightin' out through the trees and shadows the spry way that shooter done."

"I agree," said Evert.

"Maybe they had some other fella with 'em—a fella you didn't see," Danton offered. "A hunter or tracker or some such. That's how he came to be scoutin' around and found our camp in the first place."

Evert shrugged. "That's possible, I suppose."

"You damn right it is," said Elmer. "I ain't buyin' that there's somebody *else* roamin' around out here, totally aside from that bunch you spotted earlier. That'd be too much of damn coincidence. Spot this rock climbin' bunch in the daytime and then get shot at by some skulker that same night and have the shooter turn out to *not* be from the daylight bunch? No way, says I! It's those damn rock climbers we go after for payback."

"When?" Danton wanted to know.

"We find their camp in the pre-dawn and then hit 'em at daybreak." Elmer looked at Evert. "Can you find the spot you saw 'em at before?"

"Sure."

"Be nothing to it," said Remsen. "Me and Milo can lead you right to 'em."

"Uh-huh. But the thing is," Elmer said, "you ain't goin' with us."

"What do you mean I ain't goin'! Why the hell naah—" Remsen tried to rise up but then fell back as the pain from his wounded leg seared through him.

"That answer your question?" Elmer said, walking over to stare down at him. "You can't even stand, how you gonna make it through rough country in the dark and then be in shape to do anything when the gun work starts?"

"I'll cut a big branch to use for a walkin' stick. I'll tie another one to my leg for added support. Dammit, Elmer, I aim to go!"

Elmer just looked at him.

"What about Danton?" Remsen said. "He's wounded, too."

"Danton's only got a busted arm. He can shoot with the other one. And he's still got two good legs to carry him along."

Remsen gazed up, his eyes pleading along with his words. "I been right there at your side for all these years, Elmer. It ain't right to leave me behind for something like this."

"Ain't nobody I'd rather have at my side, ol' pard," Elmer husked. "But it can't be. Not this time. You'll wreck

69

your leg beyond repair, maybe even bleed to death. Besides, I need somebody to stay here and look after Virgil."

"Virgil ain't goin' nowhere. And there's nothing I could do for him that ain't already been done. If he's gonna make it—"

"He *is* gonna make it! I won't hear otherwise."

Remsen held Elmer's glare for a long moment, but then looked away. "Course he is, Elmer. Course he is."

Elmer pressed his mouth into a hard, thin line. "I've made up my mind how it's gonna be. That's all there is to it. Me, Evert, and Danton will be leavin' out about three hours ahead of daybreak. That should give us time to find the rock climbers' camp and get in position. Everybody ought to try and get some rest between now and then. Flynn and Danton, I expect you'll want to be nippin' some whiskey to cut your pain. I can appreciate that, but I can't afford for either of you to get too damn drunk, you under-stand? So, for now, ya'll go about your business however you see fit. Me, I'm goin' in to see if I can get Virgil to take some of this venison. He needs it to build his strength back up ..."

* * *

Many miles away, in the corral of an isolated scrub ranch located not too far south of the Colorado-Wyoming border, Vilo Creed strode among the half dozen penned horses, looking to pick out the best prospects for a fresh mount and two pack animals. The fact that the nearby ranch house was fully engulfed by flames at that same moment, the blaze popping and cracking, sending sparks spinning high into the murky sky, was causing the horses to mill and stamp nervously. Creed talked soothingly to them as he walked from one to the other, touching and stroking them gently.

Creed glanced occasionally over at the fire as he worked his way through the horses. The flickering light played across the flat, blank expression on his face. Only his eyes glinted with a hint of emotion as he thought about the nice young couple who lay dead inside the house. Dead and burning.

An hour and a half ago he had been taking supper with them. When he'd shown up late in the afternoon with a lame horse, seeking to purchase or trade for a replacement, the nice young couple had insisted he stay for supper and sleep the night in their stable. In the morning, the husband had promised, he would make Creed a fair deal for a replacement mount. That's where, in Creed's mind, the blame for what happened next all started. If they'd simply made the horse deal and left him to ride on, that would have been the end of it.

But to expect him to just sit there at their kitchen table, with the pretty wife swishing about all smiling and gracious as she laid out the meal, tormenting him with the way she smelled—soap and cooking aromas mixed with the woman-scent that was smoldering deep under her crisp, flower-patterned smock ... well, it was more than he could bear. It was obvious what she wanted, what she needed. A strong man, a *real* man to ride her harder and longer than she'd ever had it before.

So when Creed offered to deliver what she was asking for—laying it out plain and polite, right there in front of the husband, not like he was trying to sneak around or anything—that's when all hell had broken loose. When the

71

husband tried to order him out of the house and off their property, Creed didn't see where he had any choice but to kill the unreasonable bastard. He took the carving knife off the plate of ham in the middle of the table and, by the time he was done with it, the husband's head was left attached to the rest of his body by only a stubborn strip of spine or gristle or some damn thing that Creed finally gave up trying to hack through.

After that, he dragged the wife into the bedroom and repeatedly had his way with her. For all her teasing and egging him on, when it came down to it she just lay there like a sobbing rag doll. That angered Creed all over again. Made her just as rude as her damn husband. Even if she'd put up a fight—hell, Creed liked it when they made a scrap of it—he might have allowed her some slack. But to just lay there, limp and leaking tears, that was a damn insult. Even Jack Sampson's fat-assed old lazy squaw had bucked back with more energy than that. So, once he'd drained himself a final time, Creed went and got the carving knife again and used it on the wife, too. The strip of gristle at the back of her neck wasn't near as stubborn.

With his horses selected now and the saddle off his lame mount transferred over to the best of the three he'd culled out, Creed put the burning ranch house behind him and once more headed north. His intent was to ride through much of the night, rest a few hours toward morning, then make it to Vedauwoo sometime toward the middle of the following day.

Too bad that pretty wife didn't have more bedroom buck in her, he told himself as he rode away. Would have made for a right nice memory to carry. As it was, damn shame, all

he had was the stink of smoke and charred flesh that seemed
to linger in his nostrils long after the ranch was out of sight.

7

It was full dark by the time Cash made it back to his camp. His breathing was somewhat ragged, his right side was blood-smeared and throbbing with dull pain. The bullet that had creased him there, he knew, had cracked a rib.

Cash dropped with a heavy sigh onto his grounded saddle and wasted no time reaching for his canteen, which he tipped high and gulped greedily from. Once he'd slaked his thirst and allowed his breathing to level off, he carefully peeled away his shirt and tried to examine the wound. But it was too dark to see much more than the gash and the smear of blood he already knew was there. He poured some cool water over the bullet trough and that made it feel a little better.

"I know your pain, White Deer," came a deep, steady voice from out of the darkness. "If you welcome me into your camp, I can help you."

Cash gave a start at the words, hand instantly flashing to his Colt.

"Do not be afraid, White Deer," came the voice again. "I am an old friend who means you no harm."

Instinctively, Cash felt the urge to duck for cover. But something held him in place. *White Deer* was the name bestowed upon him by the Arapaho tribe of his boyhood. No one had called him that in years. And the voice … in spite of its unexpectedness and eerie disembodiment, there was something about it that seemed vaguely familiar and at the same time strangely comforting.

"Show yourself," Cash demanded, on his feet now, his hand never leaving the handle of the Colt. "Step out here where I can see you."

A moment later, emerging from the brushy shadows that rimmed the campsite, the frail, bent figure of a very old man eased into view. The man was dressed in colorless fringed buckskin. Various feathers were tied into strands of his long white hair. Strings of beads and bones hung about his neck, the centerpiece of these being a single large buffalo horn dangling from a leather thong not unlike the one Cash wore about his own neck.

If the man's voice had given Cash a start, the sight of him did nothing less.

"Twisted Root?" Cash exclaimed breathlessly.

The old man nodded. "Greetings, White Deer. It has been many winters."

Twisted Root had been the medicine man for Cash's tribe when he was a boy. He had seemed ancient even then.

"Come. Sit," Cash urged him. "I will build a fire."

Cash quickly weighed the risk of a fire and decided it was reasonable enough to start one. He'd already taken measures to make certain none of the robbers had tried following him and, barring that, there was little likelihood anyone would spot his fire from afar. He'd taken that into account when choosing this secluded spot, plus he'd stocked some dry twigs and branches for a smokeless burn when he first got here.

The old man nodded again. When he did so, the dangling beads and bones rattled faintly and when he moved forward in a shuffling, stoop-shouldered motion it gave the illusion that the buffalo horn and other adornments hanging from his neck were weighing him down, bending him into that posture. "Yes, a fire. It will give us warmth and light for me to tend your injury."

Cash spread one of his bedroll blankets atop a smooth boulder for Twisted Root to take a seat on. After that, he busied himself getting a fire going. Neither man spoke during this time. That suited Cash. It gave him a chance to think, to try and assemble the many questions and concerns that were tumbling wildly through his mind.

What in the world was Twisted Root doing *here*? Why wasn't he with the rest of the tribe on the reservation far to the west? Cash had gotten word several years ago that his Arapaho step father, Lightning Cloud, had died up in Canada, before the tribe was ever relocated to the reservation. Despite the differences he'd had with his father, the news grieved him. Yet, in a sense, it was better that way; Lightning Cloud would never have lasted long—and a far more miserable death it would have been for him—had he been subjected to the restraints and regulations of reservation life. Considering this made it all the more surprising to Cash that Twisted Root, who was far older than his father and had always possessed his own fiercely independent streak, was still alive.

What was more, beyond the matter of Twisted Root he now so suddenly and unexpectedly found himself faced with, Cash still had the Post Gang and the imminent arrival of Vilo Creed to consider.

As if reading Cash's thoughts, Twisted Root abruptly broke the silence. "It saddens me to find, upon my return, that the beauty of *bito'o'wu* is shrouded under the threat of so much evil."

"What evil do you speak of, Grandfather?" Cash said.

The old man pointed to Cash's bullet wound. "Those who did that to you—are they not evil?"

"They're a lawless bunch, that much is for sure," Cash conceded. "The work I do, once a man crosses that line, that's all I need to know. Whatever degree of evil may be in his heart is another matter."

Twisted Root sighed. "If not them, then another who comes. His heart is black and bottomless and the evil in him reaches all the way down."

"Do you speak of the one called Vilo Creed?" Cash asked sharply. He'd almost forgotten how uncanny the medicine man's visions could sometimes be.

"I do not know its name. I only sense that it is evil walking as a man. And you, White Deer, stand in its way."

"If you mean who I think you do, then you're damned right I aim to get in his way. It's what I came here for."

"In that case," said Twisted Root, his thin slash of mouth pulling even thinner, "you had better let me tend your wound. You will need all your strength for what lies ahead."

At Twisted Root's instruction, Cash set a small pot of water to boil on the fire. While the water was heating, the old medicine man took a needle and length of thread from one of the pouches hanging about his waist and used them to sew shut the bullet trough over Cash's cracked rib. Once the water had reached a boil, Twisted Root poured some of it into a shallow clay cup. From another pouch at his waist he took some ground herbs and berries, shredded plant leaves, a few blades of what looked like short prairie grass, and mixed them together in the steaming water. The concoction thickened into a greenish paste. After squeezing all the excess juice into a second clay cup, Twisted Root took the pulp and spread it liberally over the freshly-stitched gash. That done, he applied a direct dressing and tied it in place with strips torn from the sleeves of Cash's ruined shirt.

When he'd finished securing the dressing, Twisted Root paused and reached to gently touch the arrowhead that hung around Cash's neck. "I remember when your mother gave you this," he murmured.

"On her death bed," said Cash.

"I am pleased to see you still wear it. I am sure your mother also sees and is pleased."

Cash nodded. "That's why I'm never without it. Just as you are never without your buffalo horn."

Now Twisted Root's hand moved to rest on his own talisman. "It is the thing that reminds me how fortunate I am to have the Great Spirit in my life. It came from my first buffalo hunt. When the old bull turned to hook me and would have dragged me to the ground and trampled me, the Great Spirit reached down and caused the horn to break off and I was saved. It was a sign that told me and all who were present that day that my path from then on would always be closely aligned with the Great Spirit."

"I have heard the story many times. Indeed the Great Spirit has continued to walk close to you and speak through you over the years."

Twisted Root held out the second clay cup with the squeezings from his concoction still in it. "Now drink this," he said.

Cash reluctantly took the cup and did as he was told. The juice tasted every bit as vile as he'd feared. With the expression on his face still puckered in distaste, Cash said, "So what's going to do me the most good—the gunk you put on the outside or the awful juice you made me pour on the inside?"

"They work together."

"Good. Let's hope if the juice is as poisonous as it tasted, then the poultice on the outside will suck it back out again before it does any serious damage."

"I see the years have done little to dull the sharpness of White Deer's tongue."

Cash grinned. "Wouldn't you like to think so."

"I thought many times of our paths crossing again," said Twisted Root. "In the event that it did, I expected nothing less."

Cash's expression sobered. "Why *have* our paths crossed again, Grandfather? That is to say, what brings you back to Vedauwoo—what you call *bito'o'wu*—after all these years?"

"The answer is simple, White Deer," replied the old man. "I came here to die."

Cash didn't know how to respond to that so he said nothing, waited.

Twisted Root continued, "I have always felt a strong spiritual tie to this place," he'd said. "*Bito'o'wu* … earth-born. Born of the earth we were in the beginning, and return to the earth we all shall in the end. I always knew that, given the strength and the choice, I would come back one day and make my return to the earth here."

Cash nodded, beginning to understand.

"On the reservation, it had been more than three moons since I had a vision. I knew then that my magic had left me, that the Great Spirit was calling me home. So I came here." From the folds of his shirt, Twisted Root took a long-stemmed clay pipe and a pouch of tobacco. With a gnarled thumb, he tamped tobacco into the bowl. "I began having visions again as soon as my feet were on the soil of *bito'o'wu*. First I saw you, White Deer. When I knew we would meet again, it made me happy."

The medicine man produced a box of government-stamped lucifer matches and fired the pipe, puffing out clouds of aromatic smoke. "And then the darker visions began," Twisted Root went on. "The ones that warned me of the evil also massing here and the unsuspecting innocents in its path. That was when I knew that, before my journey could end, you and I, together, had been chosen to do battle against these evils and to protect these innocents."

"I think I understand about the evil. It is the man Vilo Creed," said Cash. "But what unsuspecting innocents do you speak of, Grandfather?"

Twisted Root puffed more smoke. "I have had many visions since arriving here. Some have been very clear, others less so. That is often the way.

"One such vision—one that has come to me more than once, yet never with complete clarity—involves many guns. Rifles. I see them being seized up by excited young warriors with faces painted for war. In my mind's ear I hear their war cries as they ride out for battle and then I hear the lamentations of their victims. But this is very brief. Next, as if from afar, I hear the thunder of many more guns and then, as the thunder grows closer, this time it is the painted young warriors who are lamenting and crying out in pain …

"It is like a bad memory, from the old times when we fought the whites and had not yet accepted that their numbers were simply too great and our way of life was destined to end. But this vision is not from the old times. It is now. Or the very near future. And the innocents I speak of are those who will be foolish enough to once again get caught up in the false hope and those who will fall victim to them before it once more ends."

Cash hesitated a moment before responding. It was obvious, of course, that Twisted Root was speaking of the guns hidden here in Vedauwoo and what was bound to happen if the Ghost Shirt hot bloods got their hands on them. When Cash spoke, he said, "You are familiar with the Ghost Dance movement that has become popular among many Indian Nation tribes?"

"I know of it, yes. Foolishness!"

"And the Ghost Shirt belief that has sprung out of it?"

"Even greater foolishness."

"If the guns of your vision fell into the hands of some young, impressionable Ghost Shirt believers, that could bring about the fulfillment of the rest of your vision."

"That would be the greatest, and saddest, foolishness of all."

"If we were able to remove the core thing meant to fuel that false hope you speak of—the rifles, in other words—it would go a long way toward *un*-fulfilling the rest of your vision."

Twisted Root puffed on his pipe, expression unchanging. "You know about the guns from my vision?"

"Know *about* 'em, yeah. They're somewhere here in *bito'o'wu*." Cash made a sweeping gesture with his arm. "Trouble is, I don't know exactly where."

Now Twisted Root's eyes narrowed. "But the evil one does."

"I'm afraid so."

"We must not let them fall into his hands."

Cash nodded grimly. "That's the general idea."

8

William Hattner paced through the cold, gray pre-dawn and cursed himself. He was on watch, walking slowly back and forth in a crescent pattern before the wagon where the others slept—the two women up in the wagon bed, Jonathan and Cory on the ground underneath. As he paced, William carried Leonard Cory's Henry repeater braced over one shoulder.

All of this, he kept telling himself, was his fault. No matter how it turned out, he was the reason they were here in this remote spot that had once seemed so peaceful and starkly beautiful but now seemed only ominous and threatening.

Even if they were able to roll out at first light, as planned, and avoided any actual encounter with the shooters they'd heard blasting away the previous evening, there would be lasting hard feelings and recriminations aimed his way. And he would deserve them.

It was he alone who had begged to make this trip after seeing Jonathan's photographs, pressuring Jonathan to crowd it in ahead of the wedding because William was scheduled to start his return trip for England immediately after and would have no other opportunity to climb these marvelous escarpments. Alice had hated the idea right from the beginning, naturally, and hadn't been shy in saying so.

But somehow Jonathan had gotten her to agree as long as it could be a "gala outing" and she could come along and bring her bridesmaid-to-be.

So now here they were. Cowering in the dark and cold, tense, irritable, at odds with one another, on guard against an unseen threat that might never even materialize.

Before sunset, Alice had announced in no uncertain terms her complete contempt for William. Jonathan was no longer speaking to him. Nor were Alice and her best friend Melanie presently on speaking terms.

What a mess.

And, providing they made it back to Denver without harm or further incident, there still would be the matter of the wedding. What of that? William had little doubt his best man role was gone. And possibly the lovely Melanie would be deprived of her bridesmaid's turn as well. But, regrettable as either of those developments might be, they would mean little as long as everyone came away safe. In that case, what William would regret the most would be if his relationship with Jonathan—his cousin and best friend since childhood— was permanently damaged.

A rustling sound interrupted William's thoughts, causing him to halt and turn abruptly toward the wagon. In the same motion he shrugged the Henry off his shoulder and brought it to a ready position. Poised in that manner, he watched a figure emerge from the rear of the wagon and drop lightly to the ground. The figure was shapeless and somewhat bulky in a long flannel nightgown but the way the silvery illumination of the waning starlight reflected off her spill of pale hair made Melanie Parsons readily identifiable. In addition to the heavy nightgown, she had a shawl wrapped around her shoulders. She drew this tighter about herself as she stepped away from the wagon and moved toward William.

"You can put away the rifle," she said in a calm voice. "It's only me."

William lowered the Henry. "Trouble sleeping?" he asked.

"Actually, I slept pretty well most of the night. I woke a little bit ago, though, and can't seem to doze back off. It must be nearly morning anyway, isn't it?"

William tipped his head toward the eastern horizon, where the first hint of dawn was starting to brighten the sky. "Won't be long."

"Have you been out here all night?"

"Cory took the first watch. He woke me to take over sometime after midnight."

"What about Jonathan?"

"I left him sleep." William shrugged. "He's already angry enough at me, I didn't feel it necessary to add to it. Maybe the extra sleep will calm him down some."

Melanie flashed a rueful smile. "I know what you mean. Alice gave me the silent treatment right up until we turned in. The way things stand, I'm pretty sure they're both equally annoyed with me."

"And the fault for that," William sighed, "I'm afraid can be traced directly to me."

"Nonsense. How are you the cause for our predicament any more so than the rest of us?"

"I'm the one who insisted on coming here to pursue my silly rock-climbing aspirations, aren't I?"

"And Alice was the one who insisted on coming along. When invited, I found the idea thoroughly exciting. I still do, if you want the truth. With you and Mr. Cory—and Jonathan, too, I suppose—I fully expect we'll come out of this just fine. *If* it turns out we truly are in any danger to begin with."

"You doubt that? Last night, when Cory suggested we take the precautions of a cold camp and the rest you spoke up favorably for the idea."

"Because it only made good sense, like I said at the time. Still, it's not like I have some deep sense of dread over the whole thing. I'm confident we'll be okay … except, perhaps, for some bruised friendships."

"Do you get the feeling, as I do," William said wryly, "that the two of us may find ourselves out of demand as a bridesmaid and best man for a certain wedding once we make it back to Denver?"

"I'd say that's a distinct possibility," Melanie allowed. "On the other hand, with Alice you never know. She and I have been friends for a long time. Her temperament is as changeable as the Denver weather. By the time we get back home and she starts gushing over the final touches on the wedding, I may find myself swept up in the mad whirl all over again. Like nothing happened."

William's expression turned somber. "I'd like to think that could be the case with Jonathan and me. But, to tell the truth, I don't know what to expect. He and I have never had any kind of disagreement before. He's very mild mannered, as you've seen. Very slow to anger. Having now reached that point, however, I fear he may be equally slow to get over it."

Melanie tilted her head and looked up at him. "This is a new side of you, William. It surprises me. Up until now, you've come across as supremely confident. Perhaps even a little cocky."

"Up there," William said, gesturing toward the towering escarpment looming up behind the parked wagon, "I am confident and, yes, I guess a bit cocky. But in other ways, like for example wielding one of these," he patted the stock of the Henry, "not so much."

"You nevertheless *look* very competent with it."

William smiled tolerantly. "I'm afraid appearances won't do much good if bullets actually start flying. Besides, either fortunately or unfortunately, this is the only firearm we have in camp. If it comes to having to use it, it will clearly belong back in the hands of its owner, Mr. Cory."

* * *

"There they are. Just like we told you," whispered Evert.

"I see 'em," Elmer grunted in response. "I also see they're runnin' a cold camp and that they got a couple lookouts posted. Them're the signs of a bunch primed for trouble, not the way a happy-go-lucky picnic party would have it set up. Far as I'm concerned, that removes any doubt these are the sonsabitches behind the shootin' back at our camp."

"Guess so," Evert had to admit.

"Plain enough to me," Danton agreed.

The three men were crouched in the shadows of a thick evergreen patch about forty yards from the climbers' camp. Elmer was centered between the other two.

The gang leader rolled his head and glanced off toward the eastern sky. "Gonna be light before long," he said. "Expect the rest of 'em will be roustin' up about then. We figure three more—maybe four, at the most—in addition to these two lookouts we can see now. Right?"

"One of those two out there now looks to me like one of the women," Evert pointed out. "I doubt she's posted as a lookout, probably just visiting with the fella holding the rifle."

"What difference does that make?"

"I'm just saying, that's all."

"Well, what *I'm* sayin' is that we got five or six people to account for. We knew comin' in there was women in the mix. I ain't crazy about bustin' a cap on a woman—leastways not a white woman—either. But if that's the way it's got to be, then that's the way it's got to be. As soon as they're up and about and we got 'em all in our sights, we set to takin' 'em down. Understood?"

"Yeah. That's what we came for," Evert allowed without enthusiasm.

Elmer looked at Danton. "How about you? You holdin' up okay?"

"I hurt like hell," the wounded man said through gritted teeth. "But I'll manage."

"You can take a couple nips of whiskey, if need be."

"I know. I have been."

"You gonna be able to hit anything left-handed?"

Danton frowned. "I don't know how I'd fare with a short gun. But with this," he tapped the long-barreled shotgun resting on the ground beside his foot, "I can damn sure do some damage as long as they're in range." He rotated his right hand, which was sticking out from the bindings that held his arm tight and immobile against his body, adding, "And with this, I'm able to reload. I did some practicin'."

"Good man. That's showin' some grit," Elmer said approvingly.

"How you want us to get in position?" Evert asked.

Elmer looked around a minute, studying. Then: "Evert, you're our best shot. You move on down a ways to that flat area. See where there's some high grass and a couple mossy boulders poking up? Me, I'll move off a ways to the left over here, up on that low hump where there's a stand of bushes. That'll put me close to where they've got their mules staked. That's how I'll start it off."

"What do you mean?" said Evert.

"I'm gonna kill the mules, that's what I mean. Put the notion of 'em havin' any chance to make a run for it clean out of those picnickers' heads right away. Then we work our way to the middle—you from the right, me from the left—choppin' down people as we go."

"What about me?" Danton wanted to know.

"You stay put, that way you won't have to move around anymore. Cut loose right from where you're at. I know you're probably out of range, but it'll give 'em something else to think about, keep 'em distracted a little while me and Evert are blastin' away. Who knows, maybe you'll get lucky and get in a few stingers, too."

"We better get where we need to be, then, while it's still dark enough to keep from being spotted," said Evert.

Elmer nodded. "Done and done. Just remember—wait for me to start it off."

9

"Wake, White Deer. Evil walks *bito'o'wu* this morning. It is not the one you call Vilo Creed, but others. The ones who shot you, I think. My vision is not clear, but my sense of it is very strong. The stench of blood is in the air … innocents will die if you do not act quickly."

Cash came fully awake in an instant. He had no recollection of falling asleep and no idea how long he'd been out. It was still dark, but the first whitish gray fingers of dawn were starting to reach above the eastern horizon.

He sat up and a faint tugging sensation on his right side reminded him of the bullet gash there. When he touched it and pressed the heel of his hand gently against it, the wound issued only the faintest twinge of discomfort. Whatever Twisted Root had treated him with had not only worked fast but seemed to have been amazingly effective.

The old medicine man sat across from him, on the same blanket-shrouded boulder where he'd perched the previous evening. As if he'd never moved. But the coals of the campfire glowed strong and red, obviously having been stoked at some point during the night.

"Where is this thing about to take place, Grandfather?" Cash said. "Where is it that the innocents you speak of are under threat from the evil?"

"I do not have a clear vision," Twisted Root said once again. "I only know that the ancient spirits who dwell in that direction," he pointed to the south, "are signaling great unrest. You must go that way. Trust your own senses. The spirits will help guide you. It is part of the reason we have been brought here, White Deer."

"Are you coming with me, Grandfather?"

"I am too slow. You must hurry. I will catch up."

* * *

Cash moved away from the Turtle at a steady trot. His eyes adjusted quickly to the gradually increasing light. He followed game trails through the brush and gullies, skirting the massive rock mounds and boulder spills, cutting across open meadows with his boots kicking the dew into puffs of fine mist.

As he plodded on, his thoughts leaped and tumbled like a buffalo stampede.

How the hell many different factions were at work here in the Vedauwoo, anyway? He had come to this remote place with the intent of intercepting Vilo Creed before he could arrange a gun transfer to Kicking Bear and his Ghost Shirt followers. So far, the marshal seemed to be running into everybody but those he'd expected to encounter—first Elmer Post and his gang of train robbers, then old Twisted Root, and now some group of "innocents" allegedly under threat from Post's bunch.

Fleetingly, Cash wondered about the accuracy of the medicine man's latest vision. He'd always maintained a healthy respect for Indian spirituality, just as he did for the Judeo-Christian teachings he had been exposed to in the white man's world. But at the same time, on a strictly pragmatic level, he also lacked total, unshakable faith in either. It seemed to him that during the hardest challenges of his life the only things he'd ever been able to *completely* rely on were his own strength and wits and the weapons he made it a point to keep close at hand.

The thought of weapons caused Cash to mentally curse the loss of his Winchester the night before in his first skirmish with the Post Gang. He still had his trusted Colt Peacemaker holstered at his hip, plus the revolver he'd taken from James Danton, now jammed in his belt for added firepower. Danton's gun was also chambered for .44 caliber rounds so he had plenty of ammunition to go around. But the added punch and distance his rifle would have given him might end up being sorely missed for more than just sentimental reasons.

Trust your own senses. The spirits will help guide you.

Despite his reservations about the spirituality that Twisted Root had so much faith in, Cash nevertheless found himself anxiously hoping for *some* kind of sign as he worked his way toward the southern fringe of the Vedauwoo. Otherwise he'd be facing a mighty long stretch of rugged terrain in which to try and find the "innocents" he was supposed to be on his way to save. What's more, if he spent too much time just poking around blindly he would be running the risk of making his presence known to the Post Gang before he had the chance to spot any of them in return.

A flock of morning doves suddenly burst into flight a short distance ahead and slightly to Cash's right. He froze in his tracks. He watched the birds rise up and pass directly overhead. Something—not him, he'd been too far back—

had spooked them. It could have been any animal on the prowl, of course. But that included the human kind. And the doves *could* be the sign he'd been looking for.

Cash proceeded across a shallow dry wash and then up the incline on the other side to where a line of aspen trees intermingled with a few cottonwoods ran across the rim of a grassy ridge. The doves had risen up out of these trees.

It was steadily growing lighter now. The first sliver of actual sunlight was only minutes away. Cash was thankful for the masking of the high grass and the shadows thrown by the trees as he eased into place at the top of the ridge.

In a deep crouch, Cash parted the grass and peered out on the fairly open expanse that stretched before him. To the right, little more than a hundred yards away, a towering, flat-faced mound of granite rose up. Near its base, Cash could see an unhitched wagon with a spill of gear around it. Close by, two people—a man and a woman, by the look of it— stood talking. They were running a cold camp, there was no sign of a fire having burned any time recently. A ways off to the left of the wagon, a team of sturdy-looking mules were staked where there was good graze.

Cash took all of this in with a quick sweep of his penetrating blue eyes.

Then his concentration shifted to what—or, more accurately, who—lay between him and the wagon camp. There were three of them. The black man was closest to Cash's position, bellied down behind some low, flat rocks with a Winchester clutched in his arms. A ways to his left, in some evergreen growth, the one they'd called Danton knelt with his left hand gripping a long-barreled shotgun; Cash took some satisfaction in noting that the man's right arm, the one Cash had busted to hell and gone, was secured tight to his body, rendering it all but useless. A short distance beyond Danton, the familiar bulk of Elmer Post was squirmed in behind a grassy hump with his Winchester resting in the crook of one arm.

Cash wondered where the fourth man, Flynn Remsen, was. He didn't like not knowing. But no matter how hard his eyes scoured the scene, he could spot no sign of the homely little gimp.

The first fiery slice of the sun was above the horizon now. More people appeared to be stirring in the wagon camp … the "innocents" Twisted Root had urged him to come to the aid of.

Cash pondered who these people might be. Experience—especially that gained from wearing a badge—had long ago taught him that nobody was completely innocent. But some came a hell of a lot closer than others. And, in this present situation, it was pretty damn clear who had the greater right to that claim.

It was also pretty damn clear that this thing was ready to bust loose any minute now. With or without Remsen, Elmer and his bunch were primed for an ambush on the unsuspecting camp.

All Cash had to do was get himself primed to stop them.

10

Flynn Remsen tipped the whiskey bottle high and let the final drops of its contents gurgle down his throat. When he lowered the emptied bottle, he discarded it with an indifferent toss over one shoulder, heard the glass shatter against the rocks.

Despite the warning from Elmer, Remsen was drunk. He'd nibbled at the bottle sparingly throughout the night, but once Elmer and the others pulled out and left him behind, he began throwing down the harsh liquor with a vengeance. And now he was drunk. *Feeling no pain*, the old saying went. What a crock. Remsen was still feeling plenty of damn pain. And he was also feeling plenty of damn resentment over being left behind like he was.

To hell with old sayings that were nothing but a crock.

And to hell with Elmer Post, too.

Remsen tried to stand up so he could go get another bottle. But the fresh wound to his leg combined with his soused condition made the act extremely difficult. He fell back three times before he got the job done, each time roundly cursing everybody and everything he could lay his tongue to. Most of all he cursed the sonofabitch who'd shot him and then, coming in a close second, he cursed not being given the chance to go after the sonofabitch for the sake of returning the favor.

Finally managing to get himself upright, Remsen began making his way painstakingly along by leaning against the boulders strewn so generously around the camp. He followed them back into the cave-like notch where most of the gang's gear was stored, including more bottles of cheap whiskey.

That was also where Virgil lay.

That goddamned Virgil. The real fault for all of this rested with him. Elmer's pampered, delicate kid brother. Stupid enough to take a bullet during the train robbery and then being so weak and wet behind the ears that Elmer, who'd been coddling the snot-nose ever since he first showed up to join the gang, had felt compelled to break all the rules and scrub their original getaway plans so they could hole up here in order to try and nurse the little bastard back to health.

In the old days, anybody who couldn't hold up their own end and threatened to bog down the rest of the gang, got silenced and ditched. Period. Plain and simple. Everybody had a clear understanding of how it was and Remsen had seen Elmer enforce that rule a dozen times.

But now, for Virgil, the tradition had been altered. What was worse, Elmer wasn't just bogging down the rest of the gang with this allowance, he was refusing to give any of them the option to take their rightful cut of the loot and move on.

That flat-out wasn't right.

Teetering now before the supply pile that contained the additional bottles of whiskey, Remsen turned his head and glared down at Virgil. Goddamned little snot-nose. He obviously wasn't going to make it anyway. A blind man could see that. They'd burn up all this precious time, waste the lead they'd gained on that stupid damn posse, and then Virgil would finally get around to dying. Why couldn't the ungrateful little bastard have the decency to just go ahead and get it over with?

A desperate thought crept through Remsen's befogged brain.

If Virgil *was* dead by the time Elmer and the others returned from taking care of those rock climbers.

Remsen shuddered so suddenly and violently that he damn near lost his balance and fell. He looked down in horror at his hands, the fingers curled as if by their own volition in anticipation of how easy it would be to clutch a folded blanket and hold it down on Virgil's face until the shallow breathing he was barely able to manage was shut down altogether. God Christ Almighty! What a repulsive thing to consider. Remsen shook his hands, forcing the fingers to uncurl, and then slapped his palms hard against the boulders he was leaning against, as if punishing them for being associated to the black deed he'd momentarily contemplated.

It wasn't that the thought of smothering a man to death was so troubling to Remsen. Hell, he'd killed men just about every way there was and never fretted one ounce over it. But snuffing Elmer's baby brother—the very one he'd been left in charge of taking care of? The thought of Elmer's wrath upon returning and finding Virgil dead—by *whatever* means—was damn near enough to startle Remsen sober. To make sure that didn't happen, he hurriedly dug out a fresh whiskey bottle with hands that had been scraped raw and bloody from slamming them against the rocks. Wrenched the cap off, hoisted the bottle, and drained several slobbering gulps.

Once he'd gotten himself calmed back down, Remsen sagged against the boulders and decided to just rest there for a while. He studied Virgil some more, his gaze softened now. *Hang in there, boy. For Christ's sake, hold on. Don't do something stupid like up and die on me. Not now. Wait until Elmer gets back and then you can kick just as soon as you want. Hell, the sooner the better after that.*

As he studied Virgil, Remsen kept looking closely for some sign of the boy's chest rising and falling with his weakened breathing. He couldn't spot anything. And was it his imagination, or did the snot-nose somehow look even paler and more waxen now than he had the last Remsen had checked?

Propelled by a new surge of alarm, Remsen pushed himself away from the boulders that had been supporting him and took an uncertain step over to where Virgil lay. He lay a rough hand against the boy's cheek and where the skin had been cool before, now it felt ice cold. The hand moved down to Virgil's chest, pressing anxiously to feel for movement from inhalation or exhalation. Nothing.

Remsen's chin began to tremble as he gave the wounded lad a shake. First very gently, then gradually rougher. "Virgil? Virgil … goddamn it, you breathe for me, boy!"

But there was no response. None whatsoever. Virgil's breathing days were done.

Remsen's wail of anguish was so loud and long that it effectively drowned out the faint crackle of gunfire suddenly discernable from somewhere on the other side of Vedauwoo.

11

Cash was unable to prevent it from starting. All he could do was react once it did.

Not surprisingly, it was Elmer who set it in motion. Without warning, he rose up and opened fire on the team of mules. With a rapid-fire rain of lead from his Winchester, he dropped the poor braying, screaming beasts in their tracks.

An instant after Elmer started shooting, the black gang member began firing on the people clustered near the wagon. And on the heels of those rifle cracks, one-armed Danton extended the long barrel of a shotgun and triggered an additional blast in the direction of the camp.

One of the campers raised a rifle and began shooting back.

Cash was in motion by then, breaking out of the trees and high grass with both pistols drawn and cocked. He hated shooting even a bushwhacking snake in the back but, under the circumstances, he didn't see where he had much choice. The black man not only was his closest target but he also was the one doing the most damage to those down in the wagon camp.

Even as Cash triggered his Colts, he saw the rifleman beside the wagon take a hit and spill to the ground. Another man ran to him, kneeling to seize up the dropped rifle. A woman started screaming.

Shooting down slope, on the run, threw Cash's aim off. His first slugs chewed into the ground well behind the splayed feet of the black man, who was stretched out on his stomach, firing with his Winchester braced across a low, broken spine of boulders. Thus warned, the shooter squirmed around to face Cash. He dropped back onto his shoulders and swung the rifle up, levering a fresh round as he did so. But Cash had his range and angle corrected by then and he never allowed the round to discharge, sending three close-grouped slugs slamming into the center of his target's chest, pounding him tight to the ground and leaving him limp, lifeless.

Cash dug in his heels, trying to slow his descent down the grassy, slippery slope now. As he did this, he twisted his torso and snapped another rapid-fire volley over at Danton, who was awkwardly attempting to shift his balance and swing the shotgun in Cash's direction. One of the marshal's bullets caught the shotgunner square in the throat and punched his Adam's apple out the back of his neck. Danton pitched sideways, instantly dead, his spasming finger touching off a final roar of the shotgun that sent its heavy load into the dirt.

Cash's goal then became to drop for cover behind the carcass of the fallen black and get his hands on the dead man's Winchester. From there he intended to finish shooting it out with Elmer.

But the gang leader promptly demonstrated he had a different plan. Before Cash could make it to cover and seize the discarded rifle, Elmer switched his attention away from the wagon camp and began pouring lead at the scrambling marshal. A bullet tore through the back side of Cash's left thigh and spun him around, sent him tumbling. He fell five feet short of the low spine of boulders. With fiery pain shooting upward through his whole left side, he immediately lunged to his feet again and made a desperate dive for cover. Another bullet caught him in midair, punching through the meat and muscle just above his left collar bone. He toppled to the ground once more, only this time he managed to roll in behind the body of the black man and his hand closed with an iron grip on the rifle he'd so badly wanted to get to.

Elmer kept pouring lead at him, slugs whining off the boulder spine and thumping wetly into the dead body. "Whoever you are, you sonofabitch," Elmer roared, "you're gonna die knowin' you picked the wrong piece of business to stick your nose in!"

Cash hunkered low and still, except for the quick, sure movement of his hands as he thumbed reloads into the confiscated Winchester. "Seems to me I'm doin' more killin' than dyin', old man," he shouted back. "I'm a deputy U.S. Marshal out of Cheyenne and you've got one chance to lay down your weapons and give yourself up or I'll see to it you end up just like your two pards."

"You're bleedin' out, you lyin' bastard of a law dog. I saw my shots hit. We'll see how tough you talk in a couple minutes when you're swamped in a puddle of your own mud."

All of the people down in the camp had swarmed to the back side of the wagon by now, using it for a shield. They'd dragged with them the rifleman who'd been cut down earlier and Cash could see his body lying very still on the ground behind a wagon wheel. The woman who'd been screaming before had now quieted to a low, sobbing wail, as if in great pain. As Cash watched, one of the men rose cautiously into view and braced the rifle—apparently they had only the one gun—over the boot of the wagon and took aim on Elmer's position. This also made it apparent they'd heard Cash identify himself as a lawman so were going to focus any armed response from their side strictly on Elmer. From what he'd seen, Cash didn't have much faith in the effectiveness of that but at least it meant he wouldn't have to worry about being fired on by them.

Elmer had gone momentarily quiet, both with his mouth and his Winchester. Cash figured that meant he, too, was reloading.

"You thinkin' over what I said, Post?" he called out. "You ready to give yourself up?"

"So you know who I am, is that it?" There was an odd mixture of surprise and pride in the outlaw's tone. "Well, if you know that much, then you know the answer to your question."

"Okay by me. Just checkin' one last time, that's all. Makes no never mind to me which way I cross you off the list."

"You figure you got time to try and talk me to death before you bleed out? Or you gonna get around to lettin' your gun do some of the talkin'?"

From his angle, Elmer must not have been able to see the man down in the camp taking aim over the wagon boot. Or maybe he was plain too focused on Cash to take notice. Either way, it must have surprised the hell out of him when a shot blasted up from the wagon camp. What was more— of equal surprise to Cash—the shot scored a hit on the gang leader.

Elmer jerked and cried out from the impact, then immediately let loose with a string of blistering curses. Cash heard the shot, heard Elmer cry out, and knew—in spite of his amazement—what had happened. The marshal snapped up immediately, raising the Winchester in the same fluid motion, intending to take full advantage of this turn of events.

Cash's eyes locked on the grassy hump where he'd last seen Elmer. The outlaw was still there but also still crouched low enough behind the hump so that, from Cash's vantage point, he was offering only a sliver of a target. Elmer was fiercely intent on triggering lead back at the shooter who'd wounded him, continuing with his string of epithets as he did so. "You rotten, dirty, no-good, dog-humpin' sonofabitch! I'll fill you so goddamn full of holes they'll be able to nail your hide up for a screen door on a shithouse!"

Cash took his shot. Then another, right behind it. Tufts of grass spurted into the air and Elmer's hat flew off. But that was all. As far as Cash could tell, he'd scored nothing more serious. By the time he levered in a fresh round and fired a third time, Elmer had broken off his barrage of both bullets and curses and pitched away from his position, rolling out of sight down behind the crown of the grassy hump.

Cash started after him and for the first time received a sharp reminder of the injuries he'd sustained when the bullet hole in his thigh caused the leg to cramp suddenly and drag him to a painful halt. By the time he got the cramp worked out, more than a minute had passed and Elmer was long gone. Trying to chase after him now, Cash told himself, would probably be futile and possibly risky since the cagey outlaw had been given time to lay a trap for anyone rushing in pursuit. Besides, even with the cramp loosened up, Cash was left feeling too damn weary and weak right at the moment to rush into anything.

It was his turn to do some cursing. Swearing at himself for missing those shots, swearing at tough, wily Elmer for punching a couple bullet holes in him and then giving him the slip.

* * *

The situation in the wagon camp was this:

Leonard Cory was dead. Alice Amberson was suffering a shoulder wound. William Hattner's left femur had been shattered by a bullet. Neither of the latter two conditions was immediately life threatening, but in both cases the bullets were still lodged in bone and muscle so the risk of further complication such as blood poisoning would become a concern before too long.

Luckily, Melanie Parsons regularly did charity volunteer work at one of Denver's hospitals and in the process had picked up some rudimentary nursing skills which now came in handy for treating her wounded companions. She also saw to Cash's injuries, plugging the bleeding and securing dressings in place. In his case, both of the bullets striking him had passed on through. Mostly only meat was torn out of his thigh, but the damage to the pad of muscle above his collar bone would require surgical attention if it were to heal completely and properly. For the time being, however, Cash knew he was going to have to gut it out and function impaired and sore.

As far as the surprise rifle shot that had wounded Elmer and helped put him on the run, the credit for that went to meek, unassuming Jonathan Kelsey. Cash had gotten quick introductions to all of the camp's survivors and made quick reads off each of them. He basically liked what he saw, except maybe for Alice, who'd obviously been too pampered all of her life. While none of them were exactly seasoned frontier types, Cash sensed the presence of enough down-deep grit in the other three to feel confident it could be called upon if needed. That was good, because he had a hunch that before this was over he might be relying on them as much as they would be on him.

Before anything else, the matter of Elmer Post had to be taken care of.

"Now more than ever," Cash explained, "I've got to go after him. He's like a wounded animal gone to the bush and it's up to me to finish him. Besides, we need the horses that I know can be found back at his camp. Otherwise we got nothing to hitch to that wagon of yours."

"Do you want me to come with you?" Jonathan asked.

Cash shook his head. "No, you need to stay and take care of things here."

"I can help with that, too," William was quick to interject. "I may be slow and lame, but I'm not completely useless."

Cash nodded. "Good. Work together. Get everything ready for when I get back with a team. We'll need to head out as quick as we can in order to get the wounded to a doctor. Cheyenne's the closest place for that."

Jonathan's gaze was flat and steady. "No offense, but what if you don't make it back?"

"Jonathan!" said Melanie admonishingly.

Cash shook his head. "No offense taken. It's a good question." He turned and pointed. "Back toward the middle of the Vedauwoo, past that line of steep rocks and slightly to the east, there's a high, round-topped mound. Some call it the Turtle. At the eastern base of that mound, in case I don't make it, you'll find my horses—a pinto and a buckskin pack animal. They ain't broke for wagon-pullin', but if you work at it hard enough you'll find a way to manage with 'em."

"How long should we give you?" Jonathan said.

Cash glanced skyward. "If I'm not back by the time the sun is noon high, start after my horses." He raked the faces before him with a somber gaze. "There are pistols and a shotgun scattered out there amongst Elmer's men. You should all arm yourselves. Even her," he jerked a thumb to indicate Alice, who lay pale and quietly moaning in the shade under the wagon. "That way, if you have to leave for my horses, Jonathan, the camp will still be protected."

Jonathan, William, and Melanie bobbed their heads in unison.

"One more thing," said Cash. "I have a friend who should be arriving before too long. He's an old Indian medicine man. For Christ's sake, don't be alarmed and shoot him when he shows up. In fact, if you give him the chance he can probably help with your wounds. His ways will seem strange to you, but they are ancient practices that have served the Arapaho people well for a very long time."

"Fair enough. We'll take all the help we can get," said Jonathan.

"His name is Twisted Root. Tell him I said to wait for me here."

12

"Goin' somewhere, Flynn?"

Elmer's voice was a low, ragged rasp, scarcely more than a whisper. But the start it gave Remsen couldn't have been any greater if the clap of doom had sounded at his heels. So intent had Remsen been on trying to mount his horse that he hadn't caught a hint of Elmer's approach. But then, considering his drunken condition—which, along with the awkwardness of navigating on a wounded, heavily-splinted leg, was the main obstacle preventing his successful ascent into the saddle—he might not have noticed the approach of a freight caravan.

While the horse continued to stand very still and patient, doing everything it could to assist in the task being attempted, Remsen had been failing at his goal for nearly half an hour. He'd painstakingly gotten the animal saddled and led over from where it had been hobbled in a patch of graze, had gotten the bulging saddle bags secured in place, but then trying to haul himself up onto the hurricane deck had been beating the hell out of him ever since. His face was beaded with sweat and smeared with dirt and dust from all the times he'd fallen to the ground. And each of those times had sent pain screaming through his leg, giving him the excuse to guzzle down more whiskey.

Right before Elmer's voice sounded behind him, Remsen had managed to climb up on top of a shoulder-high boulder from which he'd intended to try and slide over onto the horse's back and into its saddle. He was in the process of coaxing the animal around into position when Elmer spoke and nearly caused him to topple off the boulder.

"Jesus Christ, Elmer, you tryin' to make me break my neck?" Remsen wailed as he stumbled back a step and sat down suddenly, the movement painfully wrenching his leg.

"Appears to me you're doin' a pretty good job of that all on your own."

Remsen reached with both hands to massage his leg. "Aw, man, this thing is killin' me, Elmer."

"Looks and smells to me like you're keepin' it well medicated."

"You're damned right I am. You would be, too, if—" For the first time, Remsen noticed the beads of clammy sweat standing out on Elmer's face and the smear of fresh blood staining his shirt front. "Holy shit, Elmer! You been shot?"

"No other word for it. Where you packin' that whiskey bottle?"

Remsen started to reach into his jacket pocket and Elmer's Colt instantly flashed to his fist. "Make sure a whiskey bottle is *all* you pull out of that pocket, Flynn."

Remsen looked startled. "Jesus. What kind of talk is that? Why the need to pull a gun on me?"

"Just bring out the bottle. Nothing else," Elmer said. "Then, after I've had me a swig, you can back up and answer that first question I asked you."

Licking his lips, Remsen slowly withdrew the bottle of whiskey. He gave it an easy toss to Elmer who wasted no time biting off the cork and gulping down several swallows, keeping a sharp eye on Remsen the whole time. Then, lowering the bottle and slipping it into his vest pocket, he said, "Now. How about it, Flynn?"

"How about what?"

"Don't play dumb with me." Elmer wagged the gun. "The horse. The loaded saddle bags. You was cuttin' out, wasn't you?"

Remsen couldn't meet Elmer's eyes. "It's plain enough, I guess. Yeah, I was."

"How much money is in those stuffed saddle bags? All of it?"

Remsen's face lifted. "No! Just my share, I swear. Dammit, Elmer, you know I ain't that low."

Elmer's eyes blazed. "But you're low enough to cut out and leave my poor, sick, wounded kid brother uncared for and all on his own, is that it?"

"I—I heard the shootin' a while back. I knew you'd be returnin' before long. I figured Virgil would be okay until then."

"What if we *didn't* make it back? Like Evert and Danton ain't gonna do—and like I damned near didn't. You was willin' to take the chance to just leave Virgil behind and let him starve to death?"

Remsen gritted his teeth. "Wasn't no chance of leavin' Virgil to starve, Elmer. He's already dead."

Elmer's eyes darted toward the cavernous notch and then back, blazing anew. "That's a lie!"

"No." Remsen shook his head wearily. "He quit breathing a couple, three hours ago. When I made a check on him, he was already gone."

The Colt trembled dangerously in Elmer's hand. "You killed him, you sonofabitch! That's why you were fixin' to make a run for it."

"I was tryin' to make a run for it because I knew this was how you'd react," Remsen insisted. "All along you've been crazy obsessed about Virgil gettin' better and healin' up from those bullets he took—when everybody else could see right from the beginnin' he never had a chance."

"Yes, he did, damn you! He was young and strong. He was a Post!" Elmer raised his left arm to sleeve away tears of rage and grief. The Colt in his other hand drooped a little and Remsen's eyes, even in their bleary condition, locked on this and narrowed shrewdly, thinking he might have one slim chance to still make it out of this alive.

"He was soft and weak, Elmer," Remsen sneered. "You should have sent him home right at the start, never let him ride with us."

"You sayin' it's my fault, what happened to him? You bastard, you got no right to—"

From inside his jacket, Remsen suddenly pulled a large bore over-under derringer and extended it arm's length. Without hesitation he fired both barrels, one after the other. At that distance, even in his drunken state, he couldn't miss. Both slugs tore into Elmer's chest and knocked him back, staggering. As his knees started to buckle, Elmer leveled his Colt and got off one shot of his own that ripped through Remsen's lungs and splattered the rocks behind him with flecks of leaking crimson tissue.

Both men were dead before the echoes of their shots finished rolling across Vedauwoo.

Remsen's horse, having skittered away briefly during the exchange of gunfire, returned after a minute or so to stand patiently, still saddled and ready, near the boulder where Remsen's body lay.

That was the way Cash found things when he edged cautiously into the camp some time later.

13

By the time he made it back to where he'd left the others at the wagon, Cash was feeling exhausted, sore, and foul-tempered. The bullet holes in him accounted plainly enough for his physical discomfort. As far as his sour disposition, it was due primarily to being faced with the prospect of having to depart from Vedauwoo without accomplishing his main goal in coming here—to intercept Vilo Creed and prevent him from distributing the rifles cached so many years ago by Harley Boyd.

Nevertheless, chafing as coming up short on his original mission might be, Cash couldn't see where he had any choice. There simply was no time to waste getting the wounded ambush victims somewhere where they could receive proper medical treatment. Plus, it remained uncertain when—or even *if*—Creed would make it this far. Further balancing things somewhat was the consolation of being able to report that the Elmer Post gang, responsible for both the ambush here as well as the robbery of the Omaha Flyer, had been dealt with and the money from said robbery was being returned.

Cash tried to sooth his dark mood by telling himself these things. But he couldn't help also thinking that if Creed subsequently managed to get those rifles into the hands of Kicking Bear and his Ghost Shirt hot bloods kicked off an uprising that ended up claiming scores of lives, then the trade-off might not seem so justifiable.

Still wrestling with these thoughts, Cash skirted the line of aspen trees and high grass and started down the slope toward where the wagon sat. He rode astride Paint, leading his own pack animal along with two horses from the Post gang's camp, their saddle bags stuffed with the train robbery money.

The sun was high in the sky directly overhead and the day was warming steadily.

Cash had half expected he might encounter Jonathan Kelsey, already on his way to the Turtle since the marshal had been gone so long. But there'd been no sign of the young man, who apparently was showing more patience than Cash gave him credit for.

When he'd left the wagon camp earlier, Cash had had similar expectations of running into Twisted Root as he made his way in slower pursuit of his vision regarding the threat to the "innocents." Lacking that, however, Cash hadn't been particularly concerned since he knew the myriad game trails and twists and turns of the Vedauwoo terrain provided numerous paths to any given destination. He figured he and Twisted Root had simply been following different routes.

Coming in sight of the wagon again now, however, Cash was surprised to see that the old medicine man still didn't appear to be present amongst the others. Seemed curious that he wouldn't have made it here by now.

"*I am too slow ... I will catch up,*" he had promised.

Scanning the camp closer, Cash saw William Hattner seated on the ground with his back and shoulders resting back against one of the wagon wheels. The Henry rifle leaned against the wheel beside him. Melanie Parsons was kneeling nearby, her face turned away, busy with something but Cash couldn't tell what. The form of Alice Amberson was as it had been before, lying in the shade under the wagon. Seeing no immediate sign of Jonathan, Cash wondered if he had missed the young man on the trail after all.

As he proceeded down the slope, Cash's eyes flicked to either side, touching on the bodies of the two men he had killed earlier—Danton, and the black whose name he never caught. Whoever had come up from the camp to strip the men of their guns, in accordance with Cash's suggestion, apparently had felt compelled by some sense of decency to leave the bodies covered with a couple of bedroll blankets, weighting down the corners with fist-sized rocks. Proper enough thing to do, Cash guessed. But it was a damn sight more than he would have bothered with for the likes of such trash.

The marshal moved on past the bodies, leading his horses through the gap between them.

When Cash was less than a half dozen yards past where "Danton" lay, the blanket suddenly flipped back and away and—unseen by the marshal—the bulky shape of a man sprang fluidly to his feet. Although he wielded Danton's long-barreled shotgun, the shape was *not* James Danton. As the man raised the gut-shredder and took a long step forward, the only warning Cash had was a faint rattling from the numerous strings of beads and bones that dangled around the man's neck.

119

"Rein up and hold tight, law dog, or I blow you clean outta that tin star pinned to your shirt!"

The guttural command was accompanied by the singular sound of the shotgun's hammer being thumbed back.

Cash tugged Paint to a halt and froze in the saddle. He kept his face aimed straight ahead but his eyes cut hard to the left as the man moved up on that side of him. Cash already had a sinking feeling for what he was about to see. When the man stepped into full view, it was confirmed ... none other than Vilo Creed stood there aiming a shotgun at him.

Creed's broad, fleshy face split with a menacing smile. "Old Apache trick, hidin' under a dead body—or *in place of one*, as the case may be. Always wanted to try it, but never had the chance before. Real obligin' of you to leave your victims scattered around so's I could give it a try now."

"Glad I could be of service," Cash said tightly.

"You want to oblige me even more, how about you shuck your gun belt and let it slide to the ground? Real slow, it should go without sayin'. Then, reachin' over with your left hand, bump that Winchester out of its saddle boot and let it fall, too."

Cash did as he'd been told. All the while—hands going through the motions slowly, automatically—his eyes were locked on the adornments dangling from around Creed's neck. His heart hammered faster and faster as he focused on them, his mind fighting against accepting what their being there could only mean: the beads, the small animal bones, and the large buffalo horn hanging separately on its own leather thong. When Cash swallowed, his throat had gone so dry that to his ears the sound of his throat muscles working was like gravel crunching under a boot heel.

Creed saw where he was looking, was able to read his deep reaction even though Cash was trying to mask it. "The old medicine man mean something to you, did he? You'd be proud to know, then, that he died well. Old bastard was tough as salted rawhide. Course, to be fair, I didn't have a lot of time to spend on him. Had I more, I bet I could've set him to squealin' right pretty."

Cash's piercing blue eyes bored into the black, soulless ones of Creed. "Your time to squeal will be comin' soon enough … in Hell."

Creed laughed in his face. "Mister, Hell ain't got nothing to show me I ain't already seen twice over." He gestured with the shotgun. "Now ease on down out of that saddle and shake out a pair of handcuffs from wherever you keep 'em stashed."

When Cash had produced a pair of cuffs, Creed instructed him to go ahead and fasten them onto his own wrists and to "be sure and ratchet 'em real tight." Watching, the fugitive beamed with satisfaction when the task was completed. "Always wanted the pleasure of slappin' a set of irons on a law dog," he said. "Now there's another wish I can check off my list. Mister, you're dishin' out gifts to me like it was Christmas mornin'!"

"I'm in a real charitable mood," Cash said through clenched teeth. "There's plenty more I'd like to dish out to you."

Creed swung the shotgun without warning, slamming its butt square into Cash's stomach. All the air exploded out of

Cash and he sagged to his knees, folding forward, barely able to keep from pitching face-first to the dirt.

Creed leaned over and shoved his face close. "That was just to remind you who the he-bull is at this little party we're havin'. I'll let you go ahead and blow some sass—every man oughta have the chance to talk big a time or two before he dies. But make no mistake that you *are* gonna die, law dog, and there ain't a damn thing you're gonna be able to do about it."

Cash found enough air left in his lungs to rasp out, "Why not go ahead and kill me then?"

Creed threw back his head and howled with maniacal laughter. When he shoved his face close again his eyes were still dancing wildly. "Kill you so soon? Man, the party's just gettin' started and you're on tap to be the star attraction. I already had to kill the others quicker than I wanted—all except that little blonde. Me and her are engaged to be married and gonna go away together on a long honeymoon, did you know that?"

More howling laughter. Then Creed continued. "When she saw what I did to the others, she turned into the most accommodating woman you can ever imagine. Especially for such a refined-lookin' white woman—and a true blonde to boot. When she wasn't pleasurin' me with her mouth and beggin' me to do things to her that even the cheapest crib whore would never allow, she was usin' it to moan all sorts of other interestin' things she thought I'd want to hear. Tellin' me about you. And about the bank robbers and the horses and money you'd gone after ... I swear! A woman who'll drain you dry below the waist and above it load your head with all kinds of valuable information—how you ever gonna beat that, eh?"

Cash struggled to find enough air for more words. "You and her sound like a match made in Heaven ... or maybe Hell."

Creed snorted. "You're kinda stuck on that Hell thing, ain't you? Tell you what—get on your feet and get the rest of the way down there to where I can tie you to one of those wagon wheels. Then I'll give you a taste of what Hell is really like."

Cash planted one foot and tried to push himself to a standing position. But he was still cramped from the stomach blow and the leg trembled in an effort to lift.

"Come on, dammit. You were so full of tough talk only a minute ago, what happened? Get up!"

Creed's free hand grabbed Cash roughly by the scruff of the neck and yanked upward.

Cash went with the tug, the leg that had been trembling only a second before suddenly flexing with full strength and pistoning him straight up. His whole body surged, forehead slamming to Creed's mouth and nose, pulverizing lips and cartilage into a lumpy crimson smear. A bloody mist swirled before Cash's eyes. He continued bulling Creed backward, his cuffed hands knocking the shotgun arm away with a slashing blow.

Then, as Creed's feet tangled and he started to lose his balance and topple down, Cash stayed with him, jamming himself tight against the fugitive, his locked hands clawing at the strings of ornaments around Creed's neck. His fist closed on the buffalo horn—*Twisted Root's buffalo horn*. As Creed hit the ground with Cash on top of him, the marshal thrust the point of the horn into the soft pad of flesh under Creed's chin and drove it as deep and hard as he could, up behind those wild black eyes and into the squirming black mass of his evil brain.

14

It took the rest of the afternoon to make ready for departure. Inasmuch as everybody was dead except for Cash and Melanie Parsons, there was no longer any sense of urgency to get the wounded somewhere for treatment.

Cash told himself that, in her own way, Melanie had also been deeply wounded and he tried to treat her as compassionately as he could. Allowances had to be made for the instinct of self-preservation and for the after effect of shock. No one could blame Melanie for doing whatever it took to survive. Yet although Cash would never repeat the claims made by Vilo Creed, not to the girl nor to anyone else, he knew there would long be a certain stigma attached to her— perhaps by none more so than Melanie herself—for being the only one of her party spared.

After managing to overpower Creed and then freeing himself from his cuffs, Cash had gone on down to the wagon. There, he found Melanie tied hand and foot and left in the slumped, half-kneeling position he had noted (without spotting the ropes that bound her) from up the slope. After he cut away her bonds, she continued to stay slumped and silent, with her face turned away from him. He didn't know what to say to ease her torment so he refrained from saying anything at all and proceeded with the other tasks that needed taken care of.

All the bodies from the rock climbing group Cash loaded into the wagon, covering them with blankets and arranging them as gently and respectfully as possibly. Melanie neither spoke nor offered to help during any of this. She simply stood apart, staring off at something only she could see.

The bodies of Creed and the Post gang—the two up on the slope and the ones back in their camp—Cash left as they lay. Others would return to take care of them.

It took Cash a good deal of time to find the body of Twisted Root. It was in a brushy, shallow ravine about a quarter mile south of the wagon camp. As far as Cash could tell—Melanie's stony silence revealing no details—the old man never made it to join the rock climbers. Why he'd skirted *around* their camp and ended up falling victim to Creed, Cash could only guess. He imagined the old medicine man might have had some additional vision about the "greater evil"—Creed, in other words—approaching the "innocents" and had gone to intervene inasmuch as Cash was otherwise already involved.

But it was only a guess.

"... *I knew that, before my journey could end, you and I together, White Deer, had been chosen to do battle against these evils and to protect these innocents.*"

That's what Twisted Root had said on that first night when he showed up in Cash's camp. Their protection of the innocents had fallen regrettably short. But they'd damn sure battled the evils. And they'd done it together ... with Twisted Root's sacred buffalo horn claiming the ultimate victory.

Cash buried the old man's remains in the ravine, sinking him deep and covering the grave with rocks to keep away the scavengers. He said some words in the old tongue, as best he could remember.

Thus was Twisted Root returned to the earth of his beloved *bito'o'wu.*

Afterward, with dusk settling, Cash hitched up the makeshift team of horses, climbed up on the wagon seat next to Melanie, and gigged the team toward Cheyenne. It would be dark soon but Cash figured he'd have enough light from the moon and stars to travel by. For the first time he could ever remember, he wanted to get away from Vedauwoo as quickly as possible.

* * *

Two days later, Kicking Bear and a band of twenty Ghost Shirt followers arrived at Vedauwoo looking for Vilo Creed. Buzzards first led them to the bodies in the train robbers' camp and then to others, including Creed's, down on the southern fringe.

But there was no sign of the promised rifles and no clear indication of what had gone wrong here. When outlying scouts reported a sizable force of soldiers and men wearing badges approaching from the east, a disappointed and angry Kicking Bear had no choice but to withdraw and take a circuitous route back to the reservation.

Later in the year, with the snows and bitter winds of December blowing hard, Sitting Bull was inadvertently gunned down outside his tipi when he refused to call off the Ghost Dance movement, over which he had little or no control to begin with.

The shameful Wounded Knee massacre followed shortly thereafter, grimly disproving the myth of Indian garments being able to turn away the white man's bullets. After the battle, such as it was, Kicking Bear turned himself in to the Army and the whole Ghost Dance movement soon faded away.

* * *

With spring in full bloom, Cash returned to Vedauwoo.

All winter long he had worked, on and off, cleaning and polishing and carefully arranging the beads and bones on the strings he had taken from the bloody throat of Vilo Creed. The buffalo horn he'd given special attention.

Now, on the highest point of the Turtle, he climbed as far as he could go up into a sturdy pine tree and hung these items from a straight, strong bough. At the base of the tree once more, he looked out across the sun-washed peaks and escarpments of the Vedauwoo and sang in the old tongue. "My grandfather has returned to your earth, *bito'o'wu*. Now his spirit soars over you. Welcome him and treasure him … he is your son. Hold him in your embrace always."

* * *

No one ever recovered the rifles that Harley Boyd hid somewhere in the Vedauwoo.

†

AUTHOR'S NOTE

The descriptions in this work pertaining to the Ghost Dance and Ghost Shirt movements are accurate to the best of my knowledge. Same for the historical figures Sitting Bull, Kicking Bear, and Wovoka. For reasons that suited time and distance within the frame of my story, however, I took a bit of *dramatic license* and referred to Nebraska's Pine Ridge Indian Reservation in certain instances where it factually played no role.

The sporting activity of rock climbing was first introduced in Europe in the late 1880s. The ascent of the Naples Needle at Great Gable by Haskett-Smith, as mentioned in this story, was a factual event. But there is no record of rock-climbing spreading to the United States until the 1930s. Since the Vedauwoo rocks of present day, however, have come to be considered one of the world's premier climbing spots, I thought it would be fun to have some characters from my story recognize their potential about half a century sooner.

—WD—

ABOUT THE AUTHOR

Wayne Dundee lives in the once-notorious old cowtown of Ogallala, on the hinge of Nebraska's panhandle. A widower, retired from a managerial position in the magnetics industry, Dundee now devotes full time to his writing.

To date, Dundee has had nearly a score of novels and novellas plus over thirty short stories published. Much of his work has featured his PI protagonist, Joe Hannibal (celebrating over thirty years on the fictional detective scene and appearing most recently in *Blade of the Tiger*, 2013). He also dabbles in fantasy and straight crime, and lately has done some notable work in the Western genre. His 2010 Western short story, "This Old Star," won a Peacemaker Award from the Western Fictioneers writers' organization. His 2011 novel DISMAL RIVER won a Peacemaker in the Best First Western Novel category. His 2012 story "Adeline" won a third Peacemaker, again in the short story category.

Titles in the Hannibal series have been translated into several languages and nominated for an Edgar, an Anthony, and six Shamus Awards. Dundee is also the founder and original editor of *Hardboiled Magazine*.

OTHER TITLES FROM BEAT TO A PULP

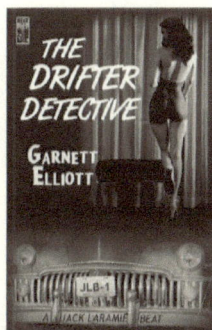

 BEAT to a PULP
PO Box 173
Freeville, New York 13068
USA
Email: btapzine@beattoapulp.com
Visit us at www.beattoapulp.com

www.ingramcontent.com/pod-product-compliance
Lightning Source LLC
Chambersburg PA
CBHW021921170626
46807CB00007B/2933